PERFECT MIX   1

Vice Club Nights

PERFECT
mix

CATE LANE

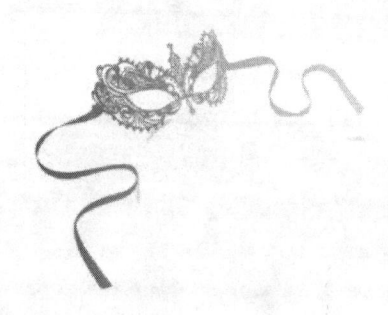

Copyright © 2024 by Cate Lane

All rights reserved.

No portion of this ebook or paperback book may be reproduced, distributed or transmitted in any form without the prior consent of the publisher or author, except in the case of brief quotations embodied in articles or reviews.

All characters and events depicted in this publication are entirely fictitious. Any similarity to actual events or persons, living or dead, is purely coincidental.

Important Note:

The following story contains mature themes, strong language and explicit scenes, and is intended for mature readers.

Cover Design by: Kim Wilson at KiWi Cover Design Co.
Formatting by: Lou Stock at L.J. Designs
Editing by: Brooklyn at Brazen Hearts Author Services
Proofreading by: Nicole at Evermore Editing

PERFECT MIX

6 CATE LANE

DEDICATION

*To All my Readers,
for their wonderful support.*

ONE
Charli

"What makes a perfect mix?" Sadie—my roommate and cousin—asks from where she sits patiently on the faded two-seater sofa, her bare feet tucked underneath her.

With my chin resting on my hand, I closely inspect the four glasses lined up on the narrow kitchen counter. "For me, it's something that is aesthetically pleasing. Nothing too pretty but more naturally understated." I stand up straight, brushing back the loose dark strands that have escaped my messy bun. "Something that teases the taste buds and has you licking your lips for more."

Picking up the first glass, I hold it to my nose and breathe in deeply, my lashes fluttering closed. "And finally, a fresh scent with hidden undertones that you can't quite name and have you involuntarily breathing in just a little deeper." A sigh slips from my lips as I blink my eyes open again. "A perfect mix should be an experience that transports you to another place. And one that you want to repeat again and again."

"It sounds like you're describing my ideal man giving me the best orgasm of my life." She stifles a giggle behind her hand. "Where do I get one?"

My cheeks lift with the full force of my smile. "Sorry, I can't help there. You know I struggle to find a decent one for myself. My track record is abysmal."

Brad, the last guy I dated, turned out to be a complete sleazeball and had me swearing off men and relationships for the rest of the year. Perhaps a bit of an extreme reaction, given it's only June.

With a shake of my head, I push thoughts of the two-timing bastard back to where they belong, filed away in the lessons-learned part of my brain. It's not that he broke my heart or anything. We'd only been dating a month. But that was long enough for me to expect he could keep his dick in his pants around other women.

Apparently, that was an unreasonable request.

For a few days after, the experience had me wondering if my decent-guy radar had glitched. But no, the flaw in Brad's personality wasn't on me; it was all him. He was simply a scumbag.

The worst part now is that we still have to work together at Lost Paradise. Another lesson learned: don't fool around with people you work with.

"Stop that," Sadie warns, no longer smiling.

"Stop what?"

"You know. I can tell you're thinking about him—the asshole. You get that lemon-sucky-face look." She waves her hand in my general direction.

A laugh bursts from my lips. Sadie's use of the English language cracks me up. "What the hell is a lemon-sucky-face look?"

"You know, like you've just sucked on the sourest lemon. Not a little squeeze, but like you sucked in really deeply. And it scrunches your face up because it's nasty."

"And that's what I look like when I think about B—"

"Don't say it," Sadie shouts, jumping up from the sofa, one cushion flying off and landing at her feet. The night I told her what Brad had done, we made a pact to never speak his name again in our apartment. She thought it was bad juju or something.

My conversations with Sadie don't often make a lot of sense, especially through the filter of a couple glasses of red wine, but that's not important. What's important is that she has the uncanny ability to be able to cheer me up in an instant. I definitely won the lottery when I arrived in New York at exactly the time Sadie was searching for a new roommate. Those first few months of branching out on my own without my twin sister Tori were hard.

Tori and I had been inseparable, always together. I could count on one hand the days we were apart. We had the same friends and played the same sports, and when we got our first part-time job while studying our business degrees at university, it was at the same nightclub.

It was difficult deciding to go our separate ways for six months, and tougher still actually doing it. Tori is currently traveling through Europe, and if it wasn't for our daily calls and Sadie's permanent state of positivity, I don't think I'd get out of bed some days. But my girls keep me sane through what has been a chaotic life for the last twenty-six years.

"Earth to Charli. Come back," Sadie says, clicking her fingers in the air.

"You know it's not him that I care about. It's working with him I can't handle." A sigh slips out before I can stop it. "I really need to nail this interview tomorrow."

Sadie skips over and squeezes me in a hug. She doesn't move in the same way as other people. It's like all the pure kindness in her heart can barely be contained, especially by the simple act of walking. As she steps back, a twinkle in her blue eyes, she delivers another of her pep talks like she can somehow read my mind the moment a negative thought takes root. "My dear cousin, you've got this. You make the best cocktails I've ever tasted, and you know I'm almost a cocktail-aholic."

"You know that's not a word. But I appreciate the sentiment."

Smiling, I squeeze her shoulders back a little tighter than usual. And temporarily, the bubble of nerves in the pit of my stomach eases, with the same effect as an Alka-Seltzer drink after a big night. I've been on edge ever since I received the email confirming the interview time. Getting this job has taken on a greater importance since the bastard-who-can't-be-named was caught screwing a customer in the bathroom where we work. I mean, seriously, he couldn't even take his sleaze somewhere else? I definitely dodged a bullet with that guy. And now I need to find a new job so I can close that mistake down completely.

Tori was the one who suggested I approach the club for a job as a mixologist. In her typical style, she'd met a wealthy guy while flitting about Europe. And during their conversation in a restaurant in Florence, he mentioned The Vice Club. It's an exclusive sex club for the elite and famous of Manhattan.

At first, it sounded suspicious. Like the guy was part of a bratva sex trafficking ring like I've read about in my romance books. She laughed when I told her that. But who meets a guy and starts talking about private sex clubs?

I worry Tori's new carefree attitude to life will get her into trouble; after all, it wouldn't be the first time. She tried to reassure me that he was nice, though I get the feeling there's more to that story than he was "a sexy Italian stranger just being friendly."

Her words, not mine.

I'm counting down the days to when she arrives in New York and I can tickle the whole story out of her.

But putting the weirdness of her encounter aside, and after a little Googling of my own later, the club proved to be totally legitimate.

Tomorrow's interview is exactly the opportunity I'd been hoping for when I moved to New York nearly six months ago. Now all that's left for me to do is prove that I can create delicious, unique cocktails like the ones before me. The four glasses I just filled stand ready on the counter, all lined up as perfectly as soldiers on parade. I'm ready to begin the tasting.

"Tell me about this club again?" Sadie asks, interrupting my internal thoughts like I'd spoken them out loud. I've no idea how she does that, and I've given up trying to figure it out.

"Well, according to the internet, 'The Vice Club is one of Manhattan's most sophisticated and exclusive sex clubs.'" I quickly drop my fingers suspended in air quotes back to the counter as I imagine my sister's voice pleading with me to stop with the air quotes. We've always been like each other's mirror. I tell her to stop frowning when she's concentrating, and she's always banging on about my air quotes, even when we're FaceTiming. I guess if your identical twin can't call you out on your annoying habits, then who can?

Keeping my hands firmly on the counter, I continue, "It's definitely not one of those blokey bars where drunk guys whoop and holler at scantily clad women dancing on a stage. I worked in a place like that back in Sydney, and I've no intention of repeating that experience."

My brow wrinkles in disgust at the memory of those desperate months trying to save enough money to leave. There's a limit to how much unwanted groping and propositioning I can handle in one night before I push back. And me pushing back turned out to not be aligned with management's thinking.

One last quick inspection of the pretty cocktails on the counter, and I take one step back. "My beauties await you," I announce, sweeping my hand through the air like I'm a gameshow hostess displaying a range of prizes.

Giggling, Sadie jumps up from where she was casually leaning against the wall. "Okay, my clever personal mixologist, where do I start?" She places her water glass farther along the counter and rubs her hands together.

With a final flourish, I drop a few fine, vibrant orange saffron threads into each glass—the only garnish needed. "This one." I hand her the first of the tall-stemmed glasses on my left. "Remember I'm trying to determine the exact measure of tang versus exotic."

She nods, and then, with her index finger and thumb holding the long delicate stem, she raises the glass high. The golden liquid dances in the light of the nearby lamp as she tilts it to the right, then left, sparking little sunbeams into the otherwise dull room. "Okay, it's certainly an aesthetically pleasing gold." She leans in, and her shoulders rise as she inhales deeply. "Yum. It smells of spicy pineapples."

"Yes, perfect. Now the taste?"

She places her lips on the rim of the glass and takes a sip before her blue eyes dance with delight. "Damn, girl, that is totally awesome. You are an Aussie cocktail wizard, and if they don't give you the job based on that, then they're idiots."

I can't hold back the grin that stretches my mouth so wide my cheeks ache. She passes the glass to me to taste and then picks up the next one. The difference between each glass is marginal. One a little stronger, with a distinct smoked-wood taste, as it contains more of the Reposado Tequila. Another fresher, with slightly more pineapple juice. And the final one with an extra dash of saffron syrup, making it sweeter but with a hint of pepper.

Sadie places the last glass back on the counter with a soft clink. "I'm feeling exotic Persian vibes. It's sexy and hot. Perfect for a sex club." She waggles her brows at me. Sadie hasn't been able to hide her amusement at the idea that I might be going to work at the club.

"A private club," I correct her, thinking me calling it that sounds better. Even after my research, "sex club" still conjures up images in my mind of near-naked women pole dancing while dirty old men tuck dollar bills into their G-strings. I have to hope the internet facts are accurate and it won't be anything like that. Or all my preparation will have been a waste of time.

Sadie picks up the last glass again and drains it. "That is so good." She smacks her lips together loudly to prove her point. "Definitely glass number four. And can I have another, just to be one hundred percent sure of my choice?"

Again, I can't help wishing Tori was sitting on the stool beside Sadie, doing the taste testing too. She's always loved these girls' nights in.

With a quick glance at my watch, I'm calculating the time difference between New York and Europe. Unfortunately, it's too late to call her now. Besides, virtual cocktail drinking wouldn't be much fun.

I plonk down on the empty stool. Tori is my other half, literally from the moment of conception, and I miss her like crazy. I'm at a crossroads in my career, which could take me to the next level or leave me having to return home to Australia a failure and no closer to my dream of opening my own place.

Unscrewing the cap off the bottle of tequila, I pour another measure into two fresh cocktail glasses. "Another cocktail, coming right up. I need to practice the recipe again anyway." I grin across the counter at Sadie, where she's perched on the edge of the stool in our small Greenwich Village apartment. "But while I pour, can you

PERFECT MIX 15

give me another of those positivity pep talks? I need to store them up in my head to replay tomorrow morning."

Her eyes sparkle with delight. "Of course. I've got plenty of them to spare."

And I don't doubt that.

TWO

Ryan

It's fucking early, and no amount of blinking my bleary eyes is going to stop them from feeling like someone threw a handful of sand in them. I lean in closer to the flickering computer screen, trying to focus on the images. It's currently split in half by a Zoom call with my business partners. One side is the face of Hunter Carlson, and the other is Gio Barbieri. They're the moneymen behind The Vice Club. Although, these days, I guess I'm a moneyman too. The club's success in the last year has surpassed all my forecasted profits and made me a wealthy man. Hunter and Gio were already obscenely rich, so they see the business more along the lines of a hobby or, as it turns out, a sound investment.

Who'd have thought my version of a private club would be so wholeheartedly embraced? Well, I did. And I was right.

The member list continues to grow with the names of businesspeople, celebrities, and the wealthy elites of Manhattan. A cross section of society who are looking for a discreet venue to act out their own personal fantasies. And fuck, they have some seriously weird fantasies. I don't think I'll ever get over my surprise at seeing some of the more serious-minded CEOs of billion-dollar businesses or high-profile celebrities doing some of the stranger fetish stuff. I'm not judging, because I have my own kinks, and private fuckery is my basic business model. Although it can be a little awkward when I see them again at one of the society gatherings that Hunter or Gio drag me to with the premise that it's good for business.

Adjusting the view on the screen, I kick my feet up onto the corner of my desk and recline as far as the large leather chair will allow. Thinking of sound investments, this chair was definitely one of mine, and I sink my aching back into its padded support. The old injury sustained from an awkward rappel down a rope suspended from a hovering Chinook tends to hurt more in the cold weather or when I'm tired, like today. Just one of my personal souvenirs of a deployment to Afghanistan with my US Navy SEALs team.

"You're looking a bit rough this morning, Ryan," Hunter observes, a smirk tilting the corners of his mouth. "Big night?" He fucking knows these early morning calls to accommodate Gio's European time zone are brutal on me.

"Are you jealous that I might have been enjoying the club's benefits while you were stuck at your desk doing boring CEO shit?" I retort. Even tired, I'm happy to join in with the usual back-and-forth banter that's a common feature of our calls.

"Don't you worry about me. I've been getting plenty of benefits of my own away from the club. But thank you for caring."

I swear his smile's turned smugger.

Blake, Hunter's younger brother and a former military buddy of mine, did mention that Hunter was seeing someone. Blake was in the 75th Ranger Regiment in Afghanistan around the same time as me. Our teams worked closely together on a few missions when we were based at Kandahar Airfield. It's hard to believe that was more than five years ago when my memories of that time remain as clear as if it were yesterday.

Trusting my life in the hands of others builds a strong bond of friendship that I'll have till the day I die. That's how I feel about Blake, and it's why I trusted him to be my seed investor. When I pitched the idea of a private club to him after leaving the US Navy, he immediately introduced me to Hunter, who subsequently introduced me to Gio, an old family friend.

Unfortunately, a year after we opened, Blake had to sell his share of the club to fund his own business plans. But by then, the three of us were in a position to buy out his share and remain equal partners.

Thinking back now, I consider myself a lucky bastard, as right from the early days of planning everything slotted into place. Gio's family owns the building that houses the club across two floors, my spacious apartment on the floor above, and a private members' gym on the lower levels. It gives us the freedom to develop the club without the need to seek agreement from other tenants. Our partnership is solid, and the guys are happy to leave the day-to-day running to me as the manager while they get on with running their own family businesses.

I fold my arms behind my head, zoning out a little as Gio and Hunter discuss something unrelated to the club. It's hard to concentrate when I'm so tired, which isn't surprising when I'm running on only two hours of sleep between the closing of the club in the early hours and having to get up for this call.

I'm seriously considering putting a large foldout sofa in my office, given the amount of time I spend here. Or, more accurately, the lack of time I spend in my actual king-size bed just one floor above. Some nights—no, I mean mornings—there's no point bothering with the stairs. It's lucky I was trained to go long periods without sleep and find it easy to grab a micro-nap when I have a spare moment.

"What's the latest with staffing?" Gio asks, his booming voice jolting me back to wide awake, I quickly focus back on the business meeting.

Unhooking my arms, I rub a hand across my eyes and sit up straighter. "Retention rates remain high, and the latest staff survey results were good. I'll email you both the report later. We do have a couple of bar-staff openings, and, as usual at this time of year, we've got people on vacation leave and a few away due to illness."

"Did you look into the idea of employing a mixologist?" Gio asks, following up from our talk a few weeks ago.

"What's a mixologist?" Hunter asks.

It's hard not to grin at Hunter's image on the screen. I like finding out there are some things the guy doesn't know, especially when most days, he seems to know everything. He's incredibly intelligent and a brilliant businessman. I'm lucky I get to benefit from his experience.

"Someone who can make fancy cocktails," Gio adds, his accent sounding thicker this week, probably due to his extended stay in Italy, where his family owns vast vineyards and olive plantations.

"It's a bit more than that. I was speaking to Tony about this. We want to offer a new menu of unique high-end cocktails. Not just the common ones you can get anywhere. But special customer-designed drinks on request."

Tony is my bar manager, a former SEALs buddy, and one of my best friends, and he already has someone lined up for an interview.

Hunter rubs his chin, then smiles. "Sounds like a good idea. I can see that would be popular."

"It will be." My words are delivered with conviction as I lean forward to prop my elbows on my ebony wood desk. I've always trusted my gut instinct. It saved my ass more times than I could count in the military, and it's made me very successful in business. "Anyway, the first interview is today. Then once we have a mixologist, I'm thinking we start them working straight away on the new menu."

The guys mutter their agreement.

"And while we're talking changes, I'm also looking to renovate the Odyssey playroom. It's the least popular with customers, and I'm thinking an adventure-themed room where we could introduce a swing would work better."

"Why would we want to put in a swing? It's not a fucking playroom for kids." Gio's image jiggles from side to side on the screen. He's obviously on his phone and striding along what looks like a back street in Florence. It's six hours ahead there, and the man never stops in one place for more than a few minutes. I swear he has undiagnosed ADHD.

With an exaggerated shake of my head, I grumble, "For someone who travels the world and is into the kinks you are, you really need to get out more. I'm talking about a sex swing."

I pick up the bottle of cold water I grabbed before the call, and gulp down several mouthfuls, suddenly thirsty.

Gio's grin is wide as he gives me a single-finger gesture. "Touchy. All because you had to drag your tired, grumpy old ass out of bed early. Anyway, you're the sexpert. Not me."

The water I was swallowing splutters back out on a laugh, spraying over my jeans like I've had a fight with a hose and lost. A rumble of laughter sounds through the speakers.

"Assholes," I mumble low but loud enough for them to hear. It only makes them laugh harder.

Hunter, through his laughter, manages to say, "Gio, you're an idiot. Even I knew what he meant, and my sexual activities are a lot tamer than yours." Hunter and Gio have been friends since school, and banter around sexual prowess is a common theme between them, though less so recently.

I do enjoy these calls—even these early ones.

"Gio, if I'm a sexpert, then you must be a sex junkie."

"Boys, boys," Hunter interjects, finally able to get his own rumbling laughter under control. "Let's agree you're both into weird fucking kinky shit and move on."

Gio and I fall silent like two naughty schoolboys being reprimanded by the school principal. Hunter is by far our self-appointed leader, even though I'm the oldest by a couple of years at thirty-six.

"Is the sex swing something to do with your ropes?" Hunter asks, bringing us back to the original point and seeming open to my suggestion more than Gio.

"No, it's not a Shibari thing, though it could be." A few more ideas for the room begin to take shape in my mind.

Hunter grins. "I like the idea."

I'm not surprised by Hunter's enthusiastic agreement, as I've been teaching him some of the Shibari rope techniques.

"And what do you think, Gio," I ask, though he's disappeared from his half of the screen. "Gio, are you still there?"

His face flashes back up on the screen. "I was just Googling sex swings. I'm in, and put me down to be the first to try it out."

"Stand in line. But you can be second. I need to be first ... for health and safety reasons."

This time, our laughter is muted by Hunter suggesting we move on to the month-end financial reports. Yet again confirming that he's the most mature of the three of us.

THREE
Charli

Damn. The weather report got it wrong again. It was *not* supposed to rain today. So much for wanting to make a good impression at my interview. I now look like a drowned rat scurrying along the Midtown Manhattan sidewalk, dodging puddles.

My chest heaves as I duck under an awning to catch my breath. From my temporary shelter, I check the building numbers to see how much further or, more importantly, how much more damage the rain will do to my person. After running all the way from the subway, I'm not sure I have much sprint left in me. Thank God I can see the entrance now, and it's only two more buildings away.

Head down, I make the final dash through the downpour, past

the two other entrances, and up the stone steps. *One, two, three,* I count, then plow straight into a solid mass of muscle. I hit so hard that I literally bounce off the man, and the owner of the impressive chest has to reach out to prevent me from landing on my butt.

"Whoa! Are you okay, there? You know you're going to hurt yourself running around in the rain looking at your feet."

No shit, Sherlock, I think but, for once, don't say. Tori would be proud of my restraint. My straightforward Aussie way of saying whatever pops into my head has gotten me into more trouble than I care to count over the years, and I'm really trying to dial it back a bit.

My eyes travel up, finally hitting high on the man's face. I peer at him through dripping strands of dark hair that have slipped out of my previously neat ponytail.

Wow.

He's hot. Not in the traditional Calvin Klein model kind of way; he's more the outdoors-man type. The kind I dream about getting stranded with in an isolated cabin in the woods. This rugged look has always appealed to me more than the pretty boys.

I inch back, and I swear it isn't to get a better look at him. Then, remembering my manners, I drag my gaze away. "Sorry," I mumble, seeming to have lost the ability to think clearly while his large hands continue to tether me to the spot. "Umm, I think I'm okay now," I add, looking pointedly at where his palms rest on my hips. Hands that are attached to corded arms and, farther up, pumped biceps that appear carved from stone and are barely contained within the sleeves of his T-shirt. We could have a Hulk situation here. And I for one would not be complaining.

He doesn't apologize like I think he should as he removes them. Instead, he looks down at me from his ridiculous height, and a deep laugh rumbles up from the chest I was just ogling. It's as surprising as it is strangely sexy.

But hey, I'm not here for the doorman's amusement, and his remarkable bulk is currently blocking my way. I straighten up to my full five-foot, eight-inch height.

"Will you quit laughing at me," I demand, before drawing in a deep, calming breath. "Look, I'm sorry I crashed into you, but I have an interview to get to. So if you would let me pass, I'd really appreciate that."

"Where is your interview?" he asks, not moving one inch. The smile he directs my way should irritate the hell out of me, given the circumstances, but when it's paired with his deep, soothing voice, it instead has me thinking all sorts of inappropriate thoughts again. This is not the mindset I need right now. If I'd run into him in another setting, sure. I would definitely be exploring this attraction. But not when he's going to make me late.

Still, he doesn't move, and I tilt my head back to deliver him my best glare. I'm too close to his chest for it to be effective, but when I take a big step backward, I trip on the edge of the welcome mat. Again, he feels the need to reach out and catch me, grabbing my hips in a way that pushes our lower bodies intimately together.

Oh my God, he feels good.

"You sure you're okay there? You seem a bit unsteady on your feet," he teases.

Brushing off his hands and dismissing his comment with an audible huff, I say with as much force as I can muster, "I'm perfectly fine. But if you could step aside so I have enough space to get through the doorway, that would be helpful."

My nerves must be causing my brain to misfire, because I'm never this clumsy or this short-tempered. Not that the doorman is helping.

Finally, he unblocks my path.

"Thank you, sir. Now if you could please direct me to the elevator." The Vice Club is on the second floor, and while I planned to arrive a little early, it's now nearly time.

"My pleasure. It's just over there." He gestures to a hallway on the left before glancing back down at me. His gaze feels like a physical touch as he scans me up and down, and I like knowing he's checking me out. I'd be a hypocrite if it bothered me after the way I've been drinking in every delicious inch of his body.

He opens his mouth to say something, then closes it again. One of his bearlike paws brushes across his short nearly black hair before he clears his throat. "First, you might want to freshen up in the restroom at the end of the hall."

Confused by his suggestion, I look down. My previously fitted charcoal blazer that I bought especially for this interview hangs limply from my shoulders, and I'm leaving drops of water on the floor where I've been standing. "Thank you, that's a good idea," I rush to say, before letting my damp hair fall forward to cover my embarrassment as I shuffle off in the direction of the restroom.

The full reality of my run through the rain hits me when I catch my reflection in a full-length mirror. Holy shit, I'm a mess. Who'd have thought a little rainstorm could do so much damage in such a short amount of time. My carefully applied makeup is smeared across my face, no doubt from where I tried to wipe the drops of water away. My hair hangs in dripping dark strands like a bunch of seaweed washed up on shore. And there's nothing I'm going to be able to do about the jacket.

Quickly, I scrounge about in my large tote. There are some out-of-date sanitized hand wipes that should, with a bit of water, remove most of the makeup, and luckily, there is a hand dryer I can use on my hair. I work to repair the damage, and in minutes, my face is makeup-free, and I no longer look like the Joker from *Batman*.

My hair is still a little damp, but at least it no longer drips, and I run my fingers through the strands one more time before redoing the ponytail.

Finally, I remove my jacket, which thankfully took the brunt of the wet weather, leaving my crisp white shirt underneath dry. Thank God for small mercies, as a wet white button-down shirt might give off the wrong vibe for an interviewee at an exclusive club.

When I walk back into the lobby, the man-wall from earlier appears to have disappeared, replaced instead with an even bigger guy standing near the elevator. He's more man-mountain than wall. Luckily it wasn't him I ran into, or I might have broken a bone.

"Ma'am, the club is on the second floor." His deep voice is Barry White smooth instead of the menace I'd expect if I went by appearance alone. He presses a button, and the elevator doors open beside him.

I mutter a thank you as I step inside and make the short trip up to the second floor. The doors ding as they open, and I fidget with the hem of my fitted black skirt that hits mid-thigh, a frown forming between my brows. It's too short. *Or is it?* I've been having this argument with myself ever since I left home. But as I didn't have another choice, it had to do.

Man, I miss having access to Tori's clothes.

Once again, I tug the hem down a little farther. I'm so damn nervous about this interview I've become irrational.

Get a grip, I admonish myself, wishing I could remember one of Sadie's pep talks. If I didn't need this job so desperately, I'd be fine. But the situation with Brad at Lost Paradise is becoming increasingly difficult as he attempts to turn the other staff against me by spreading lies.

Just as the doors are beginning to shut again, I rush out, finding myself in a spacious, opulent foyer. Navy-blue flocked wallpaper adorns three walls, and the fourth is covered entirely by antiqued mirror panels.

Suspended high above my head is the biggest chandelier I've ever seen, an impressive collection of sparkling crystals even when unlit. The foyer reminds me of the kind of sophisticated salon I'd be more likely to find in a French château than a club in Midtown Manhattan. But I like the chic boudoir vibes.

There's nobody behind the marble-topped reception desk, which isn't surprising given it's late afternoon and the club isn't due to open for a couple of hours. So I do one final check of my foggy image in the antiqued mirrors. Then, gathering every ounce of confidence I've ever owned, I pull my shoulders back and push through the super-sized ornately carved double doors.

A loft-style area opens up before me, and a huge circular bar sits across the way. I can only imagine how beautiful it would look lit up at night, all those gorgeous brightly colored bottles of spirits and liqueurs vying for attention on the shelves.

Wow, this is amazing. It's the kind of place I always dreamed of working in.

I quickly scan the rest of the space before strolling toward the bar, my shoes tapping out a beat on the parquet wood floor. It's impossible to take in all of my surroundings, but I do my best. A wide, open staircase on the left appears to lead to a mezzanine level. The dance floor, also on the left, has a small stage at one end beside a towering DJ booth. Alcoves run around the entire perimeter of the room, some angled in a way to provide a level of privacy, others more open, obviously better suited to the exhibitionist clientele.

All this, yet there appears to be nobody around. A noise from behind the wooden counter draws me closer, and when I stand on my tiptoes to look over it, I find a familiar white-T-shirted figure bent down filling the fridges with bottles of beer. Dread plants my feet firmly back on the wooden floor. Please, God, do not let the man-wall be Tony, the manager I'm here to meet.

Drawing in a deep breath, I muster as much cheer into my voice as possible as I greet him. "Hi, there. It's me again."

The guy twists in my direction, then stands. He's just as

impressive on a second meeting. And now that we're not invading each other's personal space, I'd say he's more athletic jock than linebacker. In my experience, bartenders do not look like this guy. With a tilt of my head, I try to keep my gaze on his face, even if it's almost as distracting.

"I'm here to see Tony for the interview," I say in my most professional voice.

"What's your name?" he demands gruffly. It's a little intimidating, but I'm not easily intimidated.

What the hell made this guy go from his annoying, though happier, mood earlier to this grumpy one? I brush aside the thought, still not knowing if this is who'll be interviewing me.

"My name is Charli Jones, and I'm here for the mixologist job."

This time, he appears to be taken aback. "You're Charli Jones, the mixologist?"

"I don't know what you were expecting, but I can assure you I'm her." I dive my hand into my tote to pull out the folder I prepared with my qualifications and certificates. "I have all of my certifications in this folder, and you'll have seen in my resume I've got five years' experience in—" Just as I'm about to expand further on why he should hire me, another man appears at my side.

"Charli Jones, I'm assuming," he interjects, holding out his hand to me. "I'm Tony, the bar manager. I see you've already met Ryan."

I shake Tony's hand, then spin back to the other dude I now know as Ryan. He's watching us in silence, his brows pulled down, making him look stern.

"I can take Charli upstairs so we're not in your way," Tony suggests, his eyebrow raised in confusion as he looks back and forth between us.

"No, I'll go. You stay here," Ryan commands in a deep, baritone voice, which reverberates through my body like the boom of a drum.

He steps from around the counter, moving to stand in front of me. His piercing blue eyes sparkle with humor as he looks down and says, "It's nice to meet you, Charli Jones."

He holds out his hand, and I take it, give it the obligatory shake, and then drop it just as quickly. I don't want him to think I'm interested, because I'm not. He obviously works here, and I've learned my lesson the hard way with Brad.

"Let's sit over here," Tony suggests, turning and walking toward one of the black leather sofas arranged in sets of two on either side of a low rectangle box table that I imagine is lit when the club is open.

But before I can follow, Ryan leans toward me and whispers, "I'm glad you took my advice and freshened up."

My mouth drops open with a gasp. How rude.

"Good luck, Charli," he says a little louder, then strides away chuckling to himself before sprinting up the steps, taking them two at a time.

Well, his mood improved quickly. Meanwhile, mine seems to be spiraling into panic that my interactions with Ryan are somehow going to ruin my chances.

I follow Tony, and the empty club's oppressive silence twists the threads of nerves into tight knots in my stomach.

"Take a seat," Tony offers, and I sit on the closest of the sofas, my skirt still uncomfortably wet beneath my thighs. I clasp my shaking hands together in my lap and take a calming breath.

Tony sits facing me. "We'll chat first. Then you can prepare me your signature cocktail."

We talk about my previous experience in Sydney and here in New York. He soon has me relaxing, and by the time he suggests I prepare the drink, my confidence is back. I'm in my element, pulling down bottles from the glass shelves behind me as he directs me to where each of my ingredients is stored. Once I have them all lined up on the dark polished wood, I begin.

One by one I carefully add the measures to the shaker, exactly as I practiced. The final step is to reach into my large tote and take out the jar of strained saffron syrup I prepared last night. I measure it in, add a scoop of ice, then shake it hard until the metal grows cold in my hand.

As I pour the burnished liquid into the tall cocktail glass, I explain my thinking behind the spicy, sweet concoction. Tony nods, his face an unreadable mask. I've got his attention, but that's all I can gather. He'd make a good poker player. I reach into my bag again and take out the small silver tin containing my precious saffron threads, and using the tweezers, I drop one fine strand to float on the top. Holding my breath, I place the drink in front of him and wait.

He takes a sip, then another, but still, there is no reaction. My heart sinks, and the confidence bubble I was floating on moments ago slowly deflates. But I know I did everything right.

The glass clinks as he places it back on the wooden surface, and then, resting his elbows on the edge, he leans forward. "When can you start?"

"What? I've got the job? Just like that?" I ask, unable to believe my own ears.

"Absolutely. Your cocktail was unusual, exotic, and totally awesome. I'd love to add it to our menu because it's probably the best cocktail I've tasted in years ... excluding mine, of course." He gives me a joking wink. His previously neutral expression cracking into laughter lines that fan out from the corners of his smiling eyes. Tony is probably somewhere in his late thirties, and now that his features have transformed into this friendly version of themselves, I know I'm going to enjoy working for him.

A river of relief floods my body. Only two more weeks of having to deal with Brad and his snarky comments. Two more weeks, and then I'll never have to see his nasty, cheating face ever again. I could jump for joy, but instead, I calmly place one hand on the counter, the other on top of it.

My brain switches back into gear, remembering that Tony asked me a question. "It should be no more than two weeks. I can tell my boss tomorrow when I have my next shift."

"We'll email you the details, and—"

The buzz of his cell interrupts the rest of his sentence, and he holds up a finger. "Just a moment, please. I need to take this."

He steps away, answering the call, and the only thing I hear him say is "Hey, Boss," before he's out of earshot.

Anxious nerves churn in my stomach as I chew on my bottom lip, hoping there isn't a problem. But minutes later, he's coming back.

"Charli, are you free today? I hate to ask, but we've had some staff call in sick and could use the help tonight."

With a tilt of my head, I consider my original plans for the remainder of my day. *Plans* is probably giving my trip to the Whole Foods market on my way home more importance than it deserves.

"Yes, I'm free." My tone pitches high as I struggle to keep the sizzle of excitement from my voice. "What time do you need me?"

"As soon as we've completed your paperwork?" he asks a little reluctantly.

"Oh, I guess. Um, is there a uniform?"

He glances down at my simple black skirt and white shirt. It's nothing like the thorough examination Ryan gave me, and I'm glad. "What you're wearing is fine. You won't have a uniform, and most staff just wear black. Although there is an allowance. I'll tell you more about that when we go through the paperwork."

With that, I stand and follow him through to the staff-only area.

FOUR

Ryan

My day has been on a steady decline after my early morning business call. A couple of staff called in sick, which means I was left trying to help replenish the stock myself. Then one of the beer lines in the upstairs bar was blocked, and I needed to clean it, which wasted another hour in an already hectic day. Getting my hands dirty isn't a problem, but when I have a fucking load of other business stuff to get done in my office, I'm not happy.

The only bright light had been bumping—literally—into the damp, dark-haired angel on my doorstep. At least, it *was* a bright light, until I discovered she's my new mixologist.

Apparently, she impressed the hell out of Tony with her signature cocktail in the interview. And that man is not easily impressed. If I didn't trust his judgment implicitly, I'd have asked him to look at more candidates.

Charli Jones wasn't at all what I expected. Especially when I'd assumed the person being interviewed was a guy. Thinking about it now, maybe a guy would have been better. At least then I wouldn't be sitting here remembering the moment I looked into her startled chocolate-brown eyes with my hands cradling her waist, stopping her from falling. Something clicked, or the universe shifted. I don't know what it was because it's never happened to me before. But my fingers tingled with a need to hold her tighter.

My life is black and white, with no time for shades of gray. So a tingling feeling from a simple touch was fucking weird. I have a type when it comes to women, and that type is not a pretty Australian girl full of youthful, doe-eyed innocence.

How old is she, anyway? I do a quick search through my emails to find her application and open it. *Huh.* Twenty-six. She's older than she looks. Her delicate features, with a light dusting of freckles across the bridge of her nose, had me guessing a few years younger.

With a click on the keyboard, I switch the screen to the camera pointed at the area where Charli is doing the early shift. She moves with certainty like she's already part of the crew. There were glimpses of that confidence earlier in the lobby, and I find it sexy as hell.

Very few people question my words, let alone completely disregard them. She may appear ethereal, but there is steel in her words and actions. I know that from experience. The temptation to taunt her earlier was irresistible, and the spark of fire it triggered was even more rewarding.

I watch as she laughs at something Tony said before throwing a towel to him, which he catches easily. They seem to be getting on exceptionally well for two people who only met a few hours ago.

She was only meant to help out tonight for a couple hours due to staff shortages, and already, she's been here for over three. That's the last thing I need—my manager and the new mixologist hooking up.

I saw her first.

The thought races through my mind, but I brush it away like it's an annoying insect buzzing in my head and continue to glare at the screen. I'll speak to Tony later. We don't have a no-fraternization policy for our staff, but I still wouldn't want to encourage it. Besides, it's ridiculous to think that after a couple of hours of working together, anything is going to happen between them. She's just a friendly person—unless of course, she's provoked, which was what I did earlier.

Switching the screens from the cameras to my inbox, I try to focus back on the list of fifty-four unread emails. Except, instead of reading the contents of the email I've opened, I'm still thinking about my encounter with Charli.

I probably owe her an apology. She felt the brunt of my bad mood when she walked into my club. It wasn't her fault the plumber had called to say he couldn't come as soon as she left me in the lobby. I was only restocking the fridges to work off some of my anger.

My least favorite part of running a club is having to rely on trades, who, in general, are infuriatingly unreliable. I'll be making sure the plumber never gets work from me again and make a note to find a couple new ones for next time.

That done and another five emails dealt with, I stand and walk over to the large panel of reflective glass that gives me a discreet bird's-eye view over the dance floor and one end of the main bar. I glance down and catch a glimpse of Charli's white shirt glowing in the blue light. She and Tony are standing together talking. It's not busy yet, based on the numbers on the dance floor.

Maybe it's time I was properly introduced to Charli. I can show her around the club, and it would give me the opportunity to deliver that apology.

Ensuring a new employee can handle seeing some of the club's more extreme activities is an important part of the onboarding process. Working in the main club area where Charli is tonight is relatively tame compared to the public playrooms. While some sexual acts are discreetly conducted in semiprivate, dimly lit alcoves, the group sex is specifically performed for voyeurs.

The Red Room, also affectionately known as the orgy room, requires a certain level of detached professionalism to handle. Only experienced staff work there, and Charli will be one of them, so she will need to show she can manage that level of eroticism when it's not hidden in the shadows. It's important my members are not made to feel uncomfortable for having fetishes that polite society would frown upon.

It's showtime, Charli Jones. Let's see if you're ready to see what The Vice Club provides for its members.

Downstairs, I stroll toward the blue-lit bar. Both Tony and Charli have their backs toward me when I step behind the counter and move to stand between them. Charli's gaze darts sideways, and I only notice because I'm looking for her reaction. She hasn't seen me since her interview this afternoon, and I suspect she still has no idea who I am.

Is it wrong to be looking forward to seeing her response when she discovers this is my club?

"How's everything going?" My question is directed at Tony, but I know she can hear me too.

"All good, Boss," Tony answers exactly as I expected, and I almost laugh out loud when Charli's head spins my way.

A splash of the grenadine she was pouring into the shaker spills onto her hand.

The temptation to tease her is too irresistible, so I lean her way. "Careful," I murmur.

And when she mumbles, "Sorry," while keeping her gaze hidden, I can only imagine the willpower she's having to call on to not glare at me. If this afternoon was anything to go by, I imagine she doesn't hold back her feelings very often. When faced with one of my bad moods, she flinched but stood her ground, and I admire that. It shows a strength of character that defies her tall, slim figure with legs that go on for days.

"Can you do without Charli for a bit while I show her around the club?" It's not really a question, more of a statement, and I don't wait for a response before adding directly to her, "When you finish pouring that drink."

Tony moves to take over from Charli, freeing her up to follow me.

"So you're the boss?" she asks as soon as we're out of Tony's earshot.

Grinning, I clarify, "No, Tony is your boss, and I'm his boss. A fact he chooses to ignore most of the time."

A small smile teases at the corners of her full mouth. "Okay, that's cleared things up."

I like the edge of sarcasm in her voice. She's going to fit in well.

"And I guess you didn't think it was important to mention that this was your club earlier?"

My grin broadens. "No, not really."

She shakes her head, the dark ponytail dancing over her shoulders, and I don't miss the smile that accompanies it.

"Come on. This way."

We weave our way around the edge of the dance floor toward the double frosted-glass doors on the far side of the room. I lean in close to her ear so she can hear me above the loud beats being pumped out from the speakers. "Through here are the novelty group playrooms."

She nods, and I push through the entrance, holding it open for her to pass by. A faint hint of her perfume floats up from her skin, and though it was stronger when I held her this afternoon, it has the same effect on me now. She smells of sunshine, reminding me of sunny vacations that I haven't been able to take for years. I miss being able to dolphin dive over waves or float on my back in the sea on calmer days, and the thought of doing those things with a beautiful woman like Charli has me feeling the loss harder.

The hallway beyond is quieter, and I no longer need to yell. I stop at a glass panel, one of three running along the hallway on the right, which frames the blood-red glow filtering through it from the room beyond.

"This is the Red Room."

She looks through the clear glass into the relatively empty area, but the nearly dozen people inside make it obvious that clothes are optional and sexual exploration essential.

"I guess you can see what happens here?" It's usually around midnight that things get a little wild, though tonight, the early crowd has few, if any, inhibitions left to lose.

Charli nods, but otherwise, her expression remains neutral. The only sign that she's a little uncomfortable is the vein pulsing at the side of her head.

I prop open the glass door and again let her enter before me. We walk over to the L-shaped slab of black marble that is tucked into one corner. I introduce her to the bartender, then explain that this is the only area to order drinks in this section of the club; after all, in this part of the club, the members aren't that interested in drinking. She glances around, and she could be out shopping on Fifth Avenue for all the interest she shows in the couples and small groups who are performing a variety of sexual acts on the white leather benches and beds around us.

"Would you feel uncomfortable working in here?"

"Of course not." Her gaze lands back on me, and the fiery spark in their dark depths dares me to try harder to shock her.

I'm starting to realize Charli is nothing like the innocent young woman she appears to be. With every glance, inflection in her tone, or carefully chosen words, she challenges my perception of her. And I like it.

"Good. Let's move on."

We continue along the hallway to a solid, black-leather-padded door with a gold handle. I don't open it but instead explain what's beyond—a raised central stage where groups or any couple can perform sexual acts for a small audience.

Turning, we walk back along the hallway toward the main room, and I stop at the first door on the left that we bypassed earlier. Again, I don't open it as I explain it's the BDSM room.

"This whole group-playroom area is only open on Friday and Saturday nights. Each room is monitored by live security cameras, though nothing is recorded, of course. And for the safety of our staff and members, there are discreet security guards in all areas of the club except for the keycard spaces, like the staff-only areas and the private themed playrooms on the upper floor."

For the first time, her eyes widen with interest. "There are private themed playrooms?"

I try not to imagine why this seems to be something of interest. "Yes, we have six of them upstairs. Two standard, and four themed ones—the French Boudoir, the Knight's Round Table, the Silk Road, and the Odyssey, which is about to be renovated. They're very popular, and most nights are fully booked. I'll take you up to the mezzanine level now. That's where VIPs or members can hold private functions."

We return to the main area and cross the dance floor to the staircase on the opposite side. At the top is a spacious landing with multiple groupings of tan leather sofas with low white marble cubes in the middle of them.

Charli walks directly to the closest end of the long bar. "I like this. And those chandeliers are gorgeous. It reminds me of a five-star boutique hotel lobby."

Three chandeliers hang from the high ceiling, and while I agree they look beautifully decadent, they are hell to maintain and a decorating decision I've regretted every six months when I have to hand over a small fortune to the specialist team of cleaners.

"That's exactly what my partners and I were aiming for here."

Gio had a lot of input here, which is why the furnishings are so extravagantly luxurious. He told us it was his Italian style.

"You have partners?" she asks, tilting her head in my direction, but her gaze remains fixated on the shelves of bottles.

"Two. Both are silent partners and plan on staying that way." I always like to emphasize that point to new staff in case they think it'll be a good idea to try to find out who the other owners are. Over the years, several names have been rumored, but so far, Hunter and Gio have thankfully remained anonymous. Tony is the only one of my employees who knows, but otherwise, it's a closely guarded secret.

"Any questions?" I prompt, already knowing she's not someone who tends to keep what she's thinking to herself.

She turns to look up at me. "No questions. I'm just loving the layout of the bar."

There's no doubt in my mind that Charli loves her job as a mixologist. It reminds me of what Tony said about her signature drink. "I hear you make a good cocktail."

She spins my way, a cute, dimpled smile painting her face with an innocent look that I'm getting the impression is far from the truth. "Good ... Huh. My signature cocktail is excellent."

I can't hold back my laughter at her reaction and hold up my hands in a placating gesture. "You'll have to make me one sometime so I can be the judge of that."

"You're on, buster." Her cheeks flush pink. "Sorry, I mean *Boss*."

"Charli, you can call me Ryan."

She nods, ducking her head. This woman has me constantly reassessing my view of her. It's like several personalities live within the attractive package she presents to the public, and I never know which one I'm going to get. I haven't felt the urge to understand a woman like this in what feels like forever. And it's a shame she's going to be my new employee and totally off-limits.

"Back to the staff onboarding tour. Over there are the private rooms I was telling you about. There is always a hostess at the desk, and the patrons visiting the rooms can call her to order drinks, food, and any other accessories they may want. It works a bit like a hotel concierge."

"Accessories?" she asks with one perfectly shaped dark eyebrow arched.

How did I know she was going to pick up on that one word?

"Yes, accessories. We are a private sex club. I'm sure you can guess at what I mean."

"I most certainly can use my imagination," she declares.

The problem is that now I'm using my imagination, putting various accessories and Charli together. She's a danger to my restraint, and I don't think she even realizes.

"Can I see the private rooms?"

"They are currently all occupied," I reply gruffly.

Fuck, I don't really need to see her standing in one of the themed rooms. Showing her around was a bad fucking idea. I should have left it for Tony to do when she officially starts her shifts.

Releasing my grip on the edge of the bar, I step back, creating distance between us. "That's the end of the tour. Now you should get back downstairs. It's about to get busy."

"Did I pass the test?" she asks, working out that I was checking her responses as I showed her around.

Clever girl.

"Yes." My response is short and curt. Then, before I can get caught up again in her mesmerizing gaze, I look down at my Rolex to prove the point that we are done.

She turns to face me fully, and those eyes I was trying to avoid spring wide in doe-like surprise. But I don't wait to see or hear more. Instead, I stride off toward my office, promising myself with each step that in the future, I need to steer well clear of Charli Jones and her tempting ways.

I'm the boss, and I don't get personally involved with the staff.

FIVE
Charli

Finally, my last shift at Lost Paradise is over. It's time for me to close this turbulent, unhappy chapter and truly look forward to working at The Vice Club. Those few hours on the day of my interview were fun, and the staff were welcoming, completely different from the cliquey nastiness I've had to endure here. Especially since I dared to break up with the golden boy, Brad.

The club is everything this place isn't. It's classy, sophisticated, and a lot more paradise-like than this dingy, dirty bar. At the club, no expense has been spared in creating spaces that are richly decadent. Everything is high-end, including the customers and their tastes—a mixologist's dream.

It was nice of Ryan to take the time to show me around. Obviously, he was looking for shock value. He seemed to like taunting me in that way, but I managed to mask my surprise at some of the more openly sexual activities happening in the Red Room. I'm determined not to give him the satisfaction of seeing me squirm.

I suspect he thinks I'm too innocent for his club. A lot of people make that mistake when they look at me—like Brad, who is busy serving a customer when I glance over at him. He's a prime example of one of those foolish people. But I'm a lot tougher than I look, and people only have to push me too far to find exactly where I draw the line.

Two more bottles to be put on the shelf behind me, a quick wipe down of the counter, and I'm done. I'm desperate to leave before Brad finishes flirting with the customer he just served and tries to speak to me again. My temper is a powder keg waiting for that one spark to set it off, and I'd rather not wait around for him to light it up.

However, luck has not been on my side tonight. It was bad enough that my last shift had to be spent working alongside my ex, something I'm sure he had a hand in planning. But worse than that is having to endure him going out of his way to get in my face, speaking only in filthy innuendos, and basically making my skin crawl with his deliberate brushing up against me for the last five hours. My jaw aches from having to hold in the barrage of abuse I want to spray him with. On what planet does the asshole think I would be interested in letting his dirty, two-timing dick anywhere near me? The guy's delusional.

I swipe the damp cloth over the sticky wooden surface, but just as I'm about done, two arms bracket me between the hard edge and a firm male body behind. I don't need to turn to see who it is. There's only one person who would dare to invade my personal space like this, and he's the last man I want anywhere near me. I've fucking had enough of Brad for one lifetime.

Bracing my arms on the counter, I push back hard, throwing my head back for good measure and hearing the crack as it connects with his jaw. I've never been more grateful for my water polo coach in high school, who taught me the move for when another player was reaching around me to steal the ball. There was only one time I had to use it, during a finals match against a team that was scratching and clawing at my legs under the water and out of sight of the umpire. It worked a treat, just like it has now.

Brad reels back away from me, and I turn on him. "You bitch," he accuses, gripping his jaw.

I prepare to fight if he decides to retaliate. I've stopped playing the nice girl who puts up with his shit. "You bet, arsehole. And if you lay your fucking hands on me ever again, you'll get to see exactly how much of a bitch I can be."

The other staff and a few remaining customers turn to watch the drama playing out in front of them, and this time, I don't even care. Five long hours of having to put up with Brad and his slimy moves, and my patience has stretched so thin that I can't hold back my fury for a second longer.

"You were begging for my hands on you only a month ago. So what's your problem?" he whines, still rubbing his jaw, which already has a red patch on it where my head connected.

A dark rage clouds my vision. "That was before you stuck your dick in another woman and before I knew how disappointing the experience would be." Violently waving my finger at him, I continue, "Let me be very clear because you appear to be too stupid to have figured it out by now. I never want anything to do with you ever again. Goodbye, Brad, and good riddance."

Two of the bartenders standing nearby snicker behind their hands, and Brad's mouth drops open. I push past him. His face is almost purple with anger, and an ominous shiver runs up my spine at the hate spewing from his narrowed dark eyes. I throw the cloth into the sink, wanting to run but settle on walking away with my head held high, my shoes rapping a quick beat on the wooden floor.

At the main door, my manager stands, arms folded across his chest and concern etched into his features, but neither of us speak as I stride past. He's friends with Brad and is probably worried I'll make an official complaint or something. But I've got better things to do with my time than raise a pile of paperwork that will no doubt be lost somewhere between my manager's email account and the company's head office.

Outside on the sidewalk, I draw in a deep breath, and it feels like I'm filling my lungs for the first time in months. The relief that comes with walking away is triumphant and welcome, and I pull out my cell and send a quick text to Sadie.

Me: I'm done. The sleazeball is dead to me. RIP.

Her response is instantaneous and sprinkled with emoji, telling me to hurry home because she's got a bottle of bubbles chilling and is ordering my favorite pizza.

I have two things to thank my American father for, *only* two. One was his name being listed on my birth certificate. Apparently, that wasn't a given. And the other was him having a sister who, unlike her brother, cared enough to keep in touch with us. Sadie's mother is the complete opposite of my biological father and has a hell of a lot better parenting skills than my own mother. Through my aunt and Sadie, Tori and I have found the family we always longed for.

A smile kicks up the corners of my mouth, and I quicken my pace along the sidewalk, moving away from Lost Paradise. I will never walk through that door again. As far as I'm concerned, the place can stay lost.

SIX

Ryan

She's back. And this week, I've been steering well clear of my new mixologist. Her innate goodness doesn't need to be tainted by my darkness.

From my desk, I flick through the security camera screens on my computer. *Just like normal*, I lie to myself, despite knowing the reality is that I'm looking for a glimpse of a certain tall brunette. Charli Jones has taken up more space in my head these last couple of weeks than all the women I've been with over the last five years. No, make that *ever*. She's like a drug—instantly addictive and impossible to ignore. The screen gives me a perfect view of the main bar and, more importantly, my perfect new employee as she shakes one of her fancy cocktails before pouring it into a tall glass. The dark image and blue lighting do nothing to lessen her beauty.

I continue scrolling through the other camera angles, checking that everything is running smoothly across the whole club and our guests are behaving themselves. While it may not look like there are rules, they do exist. Mostly to ensure the safety of the members and their invited guests. It's rare that I ever need to intervene, and generally awkward as fuck, so I've learned it's best to give a warning as soon as a sexual act is looking like it's getting a bit out of control. But tonight, everyone seems to be having fun, and whatever that might be depends on who the consenting parties are.

The screen returns to where Charli's working. She flicks her dark ponytail over one shoulder while smiling at something Tony just said. My gut churns at how easily they've slipped into a friendship, and while I'd trust Tony with my life, I'm not sure I could say the same about my woman's.

Not that I see Charli as my woman. But I've seen my friend break women's hearts in the past when they've wanted more than he's willing to give. And I don't want that to be her.

My head tells me to switch camera views again, but like the voyeurs at the nightly live sex shows, I can't turn away. This is fucking ridiculous. Banging on the keyboard, I switch the computer off, then scrape my chair back from my desk. At this rate, I'll gouge a hole in the plush carpet underneath before the night is out.

I snatch up my cell and wander over to the glass window, but instead of looking at the club floor below like I normally would standing here, I text Tony, asking him to come upstairs.

Shortly after, Tony strolls into my office and flops into one of the visitor's chairs. I recognize the squeak of the wheels as it shifts under his weight and don't bother to turn around from where I'm still standing at the panel of glass.

"How's our new mixologist doing?" I ask in a flat tone, still staring down at the people gyrating on the dance floor but not really seeing them.

I'm greeted by a deafening silence and turn to face him, crossing my arms over my chest.

Tony's face is painted with a knowing smile that irritates the hell out of me. That's the problem when dealing with your best friend who's known you for years and has chronicled every one of your moods and expressions. He's one of only a few who can read me.

"You seem to be taking a special interest in Charli," he responds, raising one brow before adding, "I think you like her."

"Shut the fuck up," I grumble. "And need I remind you that I'm the boss, and you work for me."

He chuckles. "Yeah, but I'm also one of your oldest friends, and I know you. You want her, but you're conflicted."

"Sorry, did I miss the part where you became my fucking shrink."

His boisterous laughter bounces off the walls of my office. "I think you're right, I might have missed my true calling. Although some might say being a bartender is half shrink some days." He continues to chuckle like he just cracked a hilarious joke.

"There's only one person here who finds you funny. And it's not me."

He doesn't need to know that, most days, his stupid jokes are what keep me sane.

"That's your problem. You don't know how to chill. I think it's great that you're interested in Charli. She's a cool girl. And let's face it, you're a fussy bastard when it comes to women."

I ignore the comment about Charli and ask, "Since when?" Seriously, I have no idea why he thinks my wanting to find a woman who's into the same shit as me makes me fussy. I have particular tastes, and it's important that the woman I share them with has the same.

"Okay then, when was the last time you had sex? I'm guessing it's been weeks, maybe even months."

"I've been busy," I answer, not even sure why I'm wasting my breath or words.

"Life's got to be pretty fucking dull if you're too busy for sex."

The scowl I direct at him appears to have no impact, and he continues to grin at me like he knows something I don't.

"I didn't ask you to come into my office so I could listen to this bullshit little life lesson according to Tony O'Grady."

"No? Then why did you call me up to your office, Ryan? Is it to bust my balls for talking to our new mixologist? Because that is not going to stop. We've started to work on a new cocktail menu, and spending time together will be necessary to do that."

Tony places his hands on the armrest of the chair and pushes up to standing. "Now, this has been fun. You know I'm always looking for some light entertainment, and as always, you delivered."

He walks toward the door, and just before he opens it, he says, "Maybe I'll show Charli the private playrooms at the end of our shift tonight. She was asking me about them earlier."

"Let's see how funny you are when we hit the mats in the gym next time," I shout after his retreating back, and the only response I get is more laughter.

There's no fucking way I'll be letting Tony show Charli the private rooms.

***

It's three in the morning, and only small groups of patrons remain. The pounding rhythms from the DJ decks have been replaced by softer tunes, and the club is winding down after another busy Friday night.

Tony and Charli are busy closing down, laughing together as they work in tandem restacking bottles, wiping down, and piling empty glasses into the three dishwashers underneath the counter.

As I approach, Tony looks up with a smug smile that screams, *I knew it.* "Hey, Boss, what are you doing down here?"

Out of the corner of my eye, I notice Charli's head turn in my direction. But I continue to focus on Tony, knowing that as soon as I look at her, my gaze will fixate on that sliver of bare skin peeking out between her fitted black T-shirt and the skintight black jeans that sit low on her hips. This is my second favorite outfit of hers. The loose black silk camisole she wore without a bra last night is by far my preference. She's only been working here officially for a week, and already, I'm ranking her wardrobe choices.

"Just doing the usual rounds," I grumble, daring Tony to call me out on the reason for my appearance when, by this time of night, I'm almost always in the office working on the club takings for the evening.

"Do you need some help?" I add, attempting to give my excuse for showing up some authenticity.

Tony's expression says everything he can't with Charli standing nearby, and instead, he agrees to my offer.

Avoiding Charli Jones has not been as easy as I thought, so in the last couple of hours, I've decided to take a different approach. I'm going to engage with her at every possible opportunity like a form of immersion therapy where the more I see her, the easier it will be to quit this ridiculous obsession with watching her I've developed.

If I had more experience in relationships rather than casual hookups, I might be better equipped to self-diagnose what it is about Charli that draws me to her.

It's not just her beauty. A parade of beautiful women comes through the club on a nightly basis, and I barely notice them. It might be the way she moves—graceful but with the strength of an athlete. Like a ballet dancer. Or it could be how good she smells. Like a breath of summer. Which I get a strong whiff of as she moves closer to where I'm stacking glasses.

The three of us work silently to close for the night. When we are nearly finished and the last of the members have gone, I wander to the curve of the counter where Charli is. "I heard you were interested in seeing the private playrooms."

She finishes washing her hands and picks up a towel to dry them. "I am. Tony said he'd show me."

Behind me, Tony coughs. "I'm sure Ryan here knows way more about what goes on in the private playrooms than I do."

The glare I shoot him from behind her back is fully loaded with enough heat to burn this place right down. I fucking want to kill my best friend, even though I know he's just messing around. Surely the judge would let me off if I pleaded that it was undue stress that sent me over the edge.

"I'm free now," I say, making it crystal clear that I'm asking to show her, not Tony.

She looks between us, her eyes coming to rest on me, then drops the towel in the basket behind her and claps her hands together once. "Let's do this ... Boss." Her voice drops low on the word *Boss*, and I feel it all the way down to my balls. My very blue balls.

She follows me up the stairs and over to Jules, the hostess who was the concierge for the private rooms tonight.

"Ryan, I haven't seen you in here for a while," Jules asserts.

I trap a groan in my throat, and the sound that comes out ends up being a low grunt. Between Tony and Jules, I'm starting to sound like some kind of kink-obsessed sex addict who likes to spend his evenings in the private playrooms. It couldn't be further from the truth. Sure, I've enjoyed the occasional evening in these rooms, and I do have my kinks. But lately, I've been too busy.

The club is becoming more popular, and membership is up 30 percent from this time last year, which means the hours I'm not sleeping, I'm in my office working. Probably where I should be now.

I introduce Charli to Jules, then shuffle her into the dimly lit hallway. Unlike the group playrooms, all of the doors here are solid wood and uniformly the same, like in a hotel corridor. The major difference between this hallway and a hotel, though, is the darker decor and the erotic gold-framed paintings that line the walls. Those would never be allowed in a public space.

Charli slows her pace to look at each of the pictures as we pass, murmuring "nice" about two of them that she appears to particularly like above the rest. I might have to come back later to take a closer look at those ones.

"I'll show you the room we're renovating first." I'm particularly proud of the way the new Den of Adventure room is coming together. Earlier this week, I emailed Hunter and Gio with the new name and photos of the progress. Hunter was on to something when he asked if it would include ropes. I think this is going to be my favorite of the rooms.

Using my keycard, I open the door and flick on the newly installed spotlight. The contractors have finished painting the walls a forest green, and the artist has begun her nighttime jungle mural. The body sex swing has also been attached to industrial-sized gold bolts in the ceiling and hangs in the middle of the room, spotlighted from above—the only light currently on in the otherwise darkened room. There are other light fittings on two of the four walls that can be on, off, or dimmed by a remote control depending on preference, but I leave them off; after all, it's the swing I want to get her reaction to.

Charli walks into the spotlight, looks up, then back toward me. "A sex swing. Now, *that* is adventurous."

She runs her hands up the ropes, and the spark in her dark-chocolate eyes has me imagining her suspended off the ground in the leather-and-rope harness while I fuck her. Looking anywhere but at her, I block the image from completely forming before my chubby becomes fully erect.

PERFECT MIX 53

My hand tightens on the gold handle, where I hover in the doorway, not trusting myself to enter the room while she's in it.

"Let's move on," I croak out of my suddenly dry throat. And when we walk into the French Boudoir room next, I go straight to the hidden mini fridge in a mirrored cabinet next to the bed and grab a bottle of water.

"Would you like some water?" I ask as Charli strolls around the canopied circular bed in the middle of the room. She nods, and I pass her one, careful to avoid our hands touching.

"This room is beautiful," she exclaims. The decor here is all royal purple and rich gold, with crystal wall sconces bouncing the warm light around the room. Three full-size ornate mirrors hang on the walls, and those, along with the mirrored furniture, make it impossible not to catch her reflection.

With a white-knuckle grip, I twist the cap from the bottle and gulp down half of it in one go. This immersion crap is not working. All it's doing is making me want her more. So instead, I think about the other rooms I haven't yet shown her, desperately needing a distraction.

The Knight's Round Table, with a Saint Andrew's cross attached to a brick wall. A round, black leather platform with various options for restraints—cold hard metal, leather, or silk rope.

Fuck, I don't think I can show her any more.

In a cowardly move I'm not particularly proud of, I pull out my cell, pretending to have just received an urgent text. And while looking down at the screen, I say, "I'm sorry, but something has come up that I need to deal with. We'll have to cut this short."

It's not really a lie, because something *has* come up. My fucking cock. And I definitely need to deal with it.

We leave, and I lock the door behind us. "You okay to get home?" I ask as we walk back toward the VIP area.

"Of course," she mutters.

Away from the tempting erotic images and play equipment that she'd look absolutely gorgeous suspended from, I feel the pressing need to touch her slowly fading, and my logical head is taking over from the one in my jeans.

I don't even know if she's into any of what I just showed her, and it shouldn't matter to me either way. Her curiosity doesn't mean she'll be rushing to make a booking in one of those rooms. She could be pure vanilla in the bedroom, for all I know, and thinking that she's a missionary-position girl helps ease the strain of my erection against my zipper by the time we reach the bar.

I finish my water and throw it into a nearby empty bin, the plastic crinkling and clanging against the metal. Charli jumps at the sound but otherwise remains silent beside me.

If only her body would stop doing the talking for her. I feel her eyes stroking across my skin, up my arms to my shoulders, and across my chest to finally land on my profile. This is what it was like that first time we met—a feeling so strong that it penetrated my skin and shot heat through the blood vessels underneath.

I turn to look down at her. And for a moment, our gazes lock. My icy blues hoping to tamp down the heat burning in her dark depths. I fucking want this woman, missionary position or any other way she'll have me. I don't care.

"I'll see you tomorrow night," she whispers, and I wish it was a promise.

I watch her run down the stairs, then stomp over to the stairwell that will take me up to my apartment.

I need a fucking cold shower after that.

SEVEN

Charli

Tony told me that the members' gym on level one was good, but this is like a candy store for a gym junkie like me. Every piece of equipment my gaze snags on is the latest, top-of-the-range model. It's by far the fanciest gym I've ever seen, and I worked in a pretty ritzy one in Sydney's most exclusive suburb when I was twenty. That now seems like the local YMCA in comparison.

The cavernous space appears to be broken up into three sections: cardio near the entrance, with treadmills, bikes, and rowing machines, then the strength area, with all-in-one trainers and benches beside towers of dumbbells, and finally, a luxe yoga studio at the far end, with black mats lined up neatly in two rows. I love my already-fantastic job even more having discovered this unexpected company perk.

But what I don't get is that the place is deserted. All this beautiful equipment is sitting idle, and the only person I've seen is the personal trainer at the front desk. Tony mentioned last night that this was the quietest time to come, but still, I expected to find at least one other person working out.

I walk farther into the gym, and the muted thwack of leather pads being hit echoes from a side door off the studio area. So I'm *not* the only person here, and curiosity has me moving toward the sound. Tony mentioned there was a room set up with thick rubberized flooring that was perfect for boxing or, in my case, practicing my martial arts moves. The closer I get to the doorway, the louder the smacking sound gets, intermingled with the low grunts of exertion coming from at least two men.

I'm a black belt in Brazilian jiu-jitsu, and from the age of thirteen, my sister and I competed in the combat sport. BJJ is all about taking your opponent down to counteract any strength or size disadvantage and then gaining dominance using joint locks or chokeholds. While I'm always running or working out to maintain my fitness, finding a sparring partner to replace my sister has been difficult. Tony has offered to spar with me, and with his former US Navy SEALs background in martial arts, he'll make an excellent training partner.

Not wanting to disturb whoever is working out, I poke my head around the doorway. My eyes pop wide at the sight of Tony and Ryan grappling on a large square of thick black matting. Both men glistening with sweat under the bright downlights. They remind me of ancient Greek statues of wrestlers fighting naked. While they aren't naked, and that's a crying shame, their white tank tops and black Gi martial arts pants display plenty of toned bare flesh. Transfixed, I watch the play of muscles across Ryan's broad back as he strains to hold Tony in a shoulder lock, the sight worthy of being captured in marble for all time. My ladybits are weeping for joy at the display of these two hot alpha males fighting for dominance.

An involuntary sigh escapes from my lips, and no reaching up to put my hand over my mouth can drag it back. Ryan's head tips my way, his piercing blue eyes making me chase the next breath to fill my lungs. But his moment of distraction is costly and works to Tony's advantage when, in the blink of an eye, he is pinned in a classic armlock between Tony's knees.

Ryan's grimace is fleeting before the words "I'm out" tumble from his drawn mouth.

Tony instantly releases his hold and rolls away. "What happened there? That last move was too easy." He obviously hasn't seen me standing in the doorway.

Ryan sits up, stretching out his shoulder, all while staring at me with an intensity that has my heart pounding against my chest wall. "I lost concentration."

I've never been someone who walks away from a challenge, and it's obvious from the way Ryan's gaze has narrowed that it's what he expects me to do.

Determined to prove him wrong, I stride forward, clapping my hands loudly like I've just watched my favorite band perform. "Nice fight, guys."

Tony jumps up. "Charli, I didn't see you there."

"Sorry, I didn't mean to interrupt you. That was pretty intense."

Ryan pulls his body up to a stand, then strolls over to the bench on the far wall. He grabs one of the folded towels there and throws it at Tony, who catches it easily, before picking up another and mopping up the sweat from his own face. I can't look away.

"I'm going to hit the showers," Tony announces, and he might as well be talking to himself for all the response he gets from us as we continue to stare at each other. It's a dangerous game that's bound to lead us to the place I promised myself I wouldn't go—his bed.

Ever since Ryan gave me a tour of two of the private playrooms a week ago, I can't stop imagining what it would be like if he truly showed me everything those beautiful, sexy rooms offered, along with some of the accessories he'd hinted at during my onboarding tour. I'm adventurous when it comes to sex, but I suspect what Ryan could offer would be an exceptional surprise-filled walk on the wild side.

My skin heats at the thought as he strolls toward me. His eyes never disengaging from mine. I've dived into their blue depths, and I'm left treading water, hoping not to drown.

"You liked watching us fight, didn't you?"

"Yes," I reply breathlessly.

"Why?"

The harshly delivered question startles me, and I blink while grasping on to it like I've been thrown a lifeline.

"Tony offered to train with me. I'm a BJJ black belt, and I need a sparring partner." I should be offended by his startled expression, but instead, I find it laughable. "What? You look like you don't believe me."

Ryan wouldn't be the first guy to doubt my ability to take them down, although in his case, and with his military background, it's reasonable that he does.

He quirks a brow. "Maybe you should show me."

"Challenge accepted," I mutter to myself while walking over to the bench to put my tote down. Bending over, I remove my sneakers and socks, then pull my oversized sweatshirt off over my head. A shiver skitters across my skin, knowing he is watching my every move, and I just might add a little extra seduction into the stretch of my arms and legs before I turn back around to face him.

"I'm ready."

His lips curl into a frown. "Is that all the warm-up you are planning on doing?"

"What do you suggest?"

He shrugs and rubs a towel across his chest, a tattoo peeking out above the neckline of his tank top. I hate that I can't drag my gaze away from his body. I've always been a sucker for ink on well-toned, thick, delicious muscles.

"Anything that gets you hot. Plenty to choose from out there." He points back into the other room.

Even though I'm already feeling really hot, I spin on my heel and follow his direction because I'm sure that's not the type of hot he has in mind. A fast ten-minute run on the treadmill gives me much-needed time to get a grip on my overactive imagination and out-of-control hormones.

Working in a sex club isn't easy when I'm on a self-imposed sex ban. Maybe it's time to rethink that spur-of-the-moment decision. Especially now that Brad is out of the picture. I don't need another relationship or a hookup with someone I work with, so Ryan should definitely be off-limits too. But one night of fun might be needed.

By the time I'm back and facing Ryan, I've convinced myself that he is just another training partner, nothing more. And if I make sure to not look him in the eye, then it might just work. At the edge of the mat, we both bow, a common practice across the various martial arts disciplines that shows trust and respect to your sparring opponent.

"Okay, show me what you've got." Again with the challenges. When is he going to learn that they only fire me up?

I waste no time and bring him down with a double leg toss then quickly put him in a shoulder lock similar to the one I saw him use against Tony.

Ryan taps the mat, and I ease my hold. "Nice work. I'm impressed, but it would have been better if you had pinned my arm to the ground so that my elbow was lower."

"What, you mean like this?" I reposition my body and reapply the lock, and he taps the mat again.

"Much better. Did you notice how that gave you more control?"

I nod, and for the next half hour, we grapple on the floor in the same way. We work through the various arm, leg, and shoulder locks, and with each position, Ryan suggests ways that I can improve my technique. He's the best sparring partner I've had since I competed in the Australian National titles when I was fourteen. Which is saying something, since my coach then was an Olympic champion.

Twisting quickly to the left, I move into the side-control position, pinning him to the ground with my weight lying across his chest. It's not easy, but I block out the feel of his muscles beneath me.

Ryan's chest rises and falls. "Now apply pressure to my shoulders," he commands, his voice raspy from exertion.

I apply the submission hold until he taps.

"Good, but from here, I can regain control by moving into the full-mount position like this," he suggests, then proceeds to demonstrate slowly until he's astride my chest, his knees high into my armpits, reducing arm movements.

Shit, his cock is right in my face, my arm pinned to my chest right against it. *Is he hard?* I struggle to draw in a full breath, not because his weight on me is preventing it but because thoughts of his thick, long cock inches from my mouth fill my head. It's impossible to look away.

Quickly, he moves me into an armbar position, and the situation goes from bad to worse. My arm is wedged between his thighs, leaving no doubt in my mind that he is sporting a fully erect cock. And it feels damn impressive pressed against my upper arm. Electric-blue eyes stare down at me, daring me to comment. Words tumble around in my head, never forming into a coherent thought, so I do the only thing I can. Tap out of the hold.

Instantly, he releases me and springs to his feet, leaving me a hot, panting mess on the mat.

"That's enough for one day," he growls, and for once, I have to agree with him.

Rolling to my side, I push up a lot slower. Already, my muscles burn from the tough session.

"Are you okay?" he asks, looking down at me.

"Sure. That was ... a good session." Out of habit, I hold out my hand to shake. It's common to bow or shake hands with your opponent at the end of a sparring match.

The hint of a smile touches his normally stern mouth when his large hand swallows up mine. Heat floods my body—not the kind I feel after doing strenuous exercise, but the kind that zaps through my nerve endings, making them supersensitive to the lightest of touches. I can't help wondering what it would feel like to have his hot palm against other parts of my body.

Still holding my hand, Ryan says, "There is a cold tub on the other side of the locker room if you want to prevent muscle soreness tomorrow."

"I might just do that." Reclaiming my hand, I move over to the bench and grab a fresh towel from the neatly folded stack. Perspiration runs in rivulets down my body, and the idea of an ice bath sounds perfect. With my back to Ryan, I'm more capable of processing thoughts. I pick up my shoes and stuff them into my bag before slinging it over my shoulder.

More composed, I turn to face my hot boss—a point I really need to remember.

He's. My. Boss.

"Thank you for sparring with me. It's been a while, and I appreciate all the tips. Maybe we can do it again sometime?"

His scowl is back in full force, with his jaw clenched and his forehead contorted into deep frown lines.

"Or I could ask Tony," I backtrack, unsure if asking him to train with me again would be a bit presumptuous; after all, he's a very busy man running the club.

"No," he barks at me, then softens his tone and adds, "I'll spar with you."

"Okay. Umm, just let me know when you have time," I reply before escaping.

EIGHT

Ryan

Golden liquid swirls around in the base of the crystal glass as I tilt it from side to side. I have a pile of work to do, but instead, I'm hiding in my office, drinking a JD and avoiding a certain woman who I can't get the fuck out of my head.

Charli is not just another attractive girl working in my club. Nor is she the first Australian we've employed; Rob, the DJ, is from Sydney. No, there is something about the gorgeous brunette that's different—special—and I just can't put my finger on it. A strength of mind and body all wrapped up in a sexy package.

Fuck, when she removed her sweatshirt to reveal her full breasts squeezed into a tiny hot-pink crop top, I should have known right then that sparring with her was going to be a bad idea. And I was right.

Every movement felt like a form of foreplay, from the side-control position, where she lay across my chest, pushing those luscious breasts up so they spilled over the neckline of that ridiculously small top, to the back mount, where she attached her body to my back and hooked her strong, toned thighs around me. Fucking her would be something else with that kind of strength and flexibility.

Until now, I'd only ever sparred with guys, the opportunity to match my skills to a woman never coming up. But if that wasn't the hottest fucking thing, grappling with Charli on the mats, then I don't know what else could be. Hold it. Maybe I can think of something better. Wrapping Charli's gorgeous curves up in silk ropes.

I've been practicing Shibari for five years. But in all my use of rope play to provide a sensual and emotional experience for my sexual partner, I've never felt as strong a desire to see a woman bound and watch her expression the moment the knots touch her bare skin.

I close my eyes, remembering the way her body pressed against mine, beneath me, around me, and under me. It's not surprising I got an erection. I'm getting one now just thinking about the feel of her sweat-slicked skin.

My computer screen pings with an incoming call, requesting me to join a Zoom with Hunter and Gio.

Fuck, I completely lost track of time. The monthly call was due to start ten minutes ago, and the worst part is, it was me who begged them to do the late-afternoon time rather than tomorrow morning. I connect to the call, and Hunter and Gio appear on the split screen.

Hunter is already scowling. "You're late." He's obviously had a bad day, though I can't blame him for being pissed. I hate people being late too.

"Sorry, man. The time got away from me."

"It doesn't have anything to do with the glass of whiskey I can see in your hand?" Gio chimes in, not really helping.

Of course the whiskey had everything to do with turning off thoughts of Charli, but I'm not about to admit this to them. "Feel free to join me. Virtually, of course."

"It's not a bad idea," Hunter grumbles, reaching down, then bringing up a bottle of Macallan. Of course he wouldn't be drinking the cheap stuff.

"I'm afraid I can't join in. Although I could do with a drink, as I've been summoned to dinner with my father."

Gio's relationship with his father has been a difficult one. While the senior Barbieri has handed over the role of CEO to Gio, he seems reluctant to give his son any of the control that goes along with it. It's one of the reasons Gio has had to spend more time in Florence these last six months despite his penthouse on Fifth Avenue being his home base. From an outsider's point of view, it feels like the two men are heading for a major clash. And that's never going to end well when it's family.

Maybe growing up an only child who was passed back and forth between my drug-addicted mother and elderly grandparents, who have now both sadly passed, wasn't so bad after all.

"If there's anything I can do to help," I offer, knowing he's unlikely to take me up on it. He has never asked for help in the past, and I can't see him doing it now.

"Same, man," Hunter adds before taking a sip of his drink. The frown lines don't seem as deep as they were.

"Thanks. But this is something my father and I have to work out." Gio turns his head to the side for a minute, resting it against the black leather headrest of a car. "Look, guys. I probably have to go soon. Just to let you know, I emailed through my approval of the additional funds for the renovation and last month's financials. Is there anything else you need from me?"

On my second screen, I scan through the minutes from our last meeting. "No, Gio, that's all the decisions I needed. But are you still planning on coming back in a couple of weeks?"

"Yes, I'll send you both the dates. Unfortunately, it will have to be a brief visit. But hopefully, that will change in a couple of months. Why, do you miss me?"

Hunter and I are quick to deny any claims of missing him. What I don't add is that the thing I do miss about my friend is his lighthearted banter, and I know Hunter feels the same. These last few weeks, Gio hasn't been his usual annoying, chirpy self.

Gio ends the call, leaving Hunter and I to chat for a little longer. He has a special night planned for a woman, and he needs some help learning some of the Shibari knots he'd like to try.

"Blake told me you were seeing someone."

He smiles. "Trudy works for him and is his girlfriend's best friend. We've kind of had this friends-with-benefits thing going on for a few months."

A wheezing cough bursts from my mouth. "I didn't realize that actually happened outside the club." I smirk and tip my glass toward the screen, and he does the same, returning my mirth with a virtual cheers of his own.

He smiles, looking a lot happier talking about this new woman. "It does, and it's been good, but now I'm thinking I'd like to make the arrangement more like a proper relationship."

"And that includes bringing her to the club?" I'm a little surprised he thinks a visit to the club would be the way to impress a woman. Surely, a weekend at his family's beach house in Southampton would be more appropriate. But what do I know?

He laughs. "No, that's just purely for pleasure. I think she'll like what I have planned."

In all the time I've known Hunter, he's never been this interested in a woman. I'm happy for him, and maybe just a little envious. Which gets me thinking …

"Hey, I've got a question. If I was thinking of taking a girl out for the first time, where should I take her?"

This time he's the one left coughing after a sip of his drink. "What? You dating?"

My scowl is back in full force and directed at his virtual image. "Asshole," I mumble. "Call it a hypothetical. I did say *if*."

His smirk tempts me to disconnect the Zoom call. The problem is I want to know his answer. Hunter knows more about dating women than me, even with his current situation. I've been a casual-hookup guy for so long that I can't remember the last time I went on a date. Fuck, it was probably back in high school.

Once I'd signed up for the US Navy, I was never in one place long enough for the idea of dating to take hold. I'd meet a woman at a local bar, and if I wanted to see her again, I'd let her know where I'd be the next night. Looking back, I was an arrogant asshole. But at that time in my life, I didn't want to commit to anyone. It wouldn't have been right when I was risking my life from one mission to the next.

"Sorry, you just surprised me. I'm no expert, because I can't even convince my woman to go on a date with me, but for a first date, hypothetically"—he grins—"I'd suggest keeping it simple with dinner at a nice restaurant. And if you really want to impress, pick a place like Leonardo's." His suggestion of Gio's brother's restaurant is a good one. The wait list is generally more than a month long, but Leo always comes through for us when we need a table on short notice.

"Thanks, man. I appreciate it."

Not long after, we finish our drinks and end the call.

The idea of dating Charli doesn't concern me. It's doing it right that does. And more importantly, the fact that she may not want to go on a date with a guy my age. That thought sits heavy on my shoulders. And I guess that's where I'm at.

Yes, it's too soon to be thinking about asking her on a date, and I pour myself another drink to wash the idea away.

NINE

Charli

It's early evening by the time I'm skipping up the stone steps of The Vice Club. A grin stretches across my face like it's done every time since the first day I started working here.

Noticing the older couple walking their dog across the street in this swanky part of the city, I wonder if they know what lies behind the unassuming facade of this building. The last thing I expect they'd say is a private sex club.

Before I even reach the top step, the large black door is swung open, and Mario, the doorman, fills the opening.

"Hey, Charli. How you doing?" The six-foot-seven Italian man-mountain greets me in his strong Bronx accent. Initially, I was intimidated by his bulk, but as time has rolled on and I've gotten to know him, I've realized he's more a big teddy bear than scary. Don't get me wrong, Mario could be scary if he wanted to be, but with me, he's sweet.

"Fine, thanks, Mario. Tell me, did your son enjoy his birthday treat?" Yesterday, he was telling me it was his son's fifth birthday, and he and his wife were taking him to the Bronx Zoo today.

"He did. That kid loves animals." His toothy, lopsided grin spreads his cheeks wide and has me smiling back up at him.

"I'll have to go myself one day. Maybe when my sister arrives in a couple of weeks."

He nods, swiping his keycard to call the elevator before I've had a chance to get mine out from the depths of my tote.

It arrives with a ding, and I step into the cab. "See you later, Mario."

It looks busy tonight when I push through the door into the main part of the club, the bright blue lights immediately drawing my eye as I suspect they do for every visitor. I love seeing it all lit up like the Rockefeller Center Christmas tree. Tonight I'll be working in the VIP bar upstairs. It will be my first time, and I'm looking forward to it.

Tony texted me earlier to say there were a couple of celebrities dropping in tonight, and Ryan thought they'd appreciate my custom cocktails. A swell of pride fills my chest. The new cocktail menu Tony and I worked on is proving to be very popular with the members—especially my signature mix. It seems even Ryan has noticed.

A master dom strolls past in head-to-toe leather with a feathered mask, proudly leading her sub across the room and up the staircase. I don't really get that submissive-dominance kind of thing, but hey, if it makes them happy, good on them.

Waiters and waitresses flash past in brightly colored sequined costumes as I stroll to the staff-only entrance. I say hi to each of them, as over the last couple of weeks, I've managed to meet everyone. They've all been really friendly, and what's even better is that I've not heard a bad word said about anyone. The complete opposite of Lost Paradise.

Using my keycard, I push through into the silent hallway, leaving the heavy beat of dance music behind on the other side of the soundproofed door. The only noise now the click of my heels against the hard floor. A few moments of peace left to relish before starting my shift. I really feel like I've found my place—not just here at the club, with a growing circle of new friends, but in this big, overwhelming city.

***

Tonight's celebrities turn out to be Chris Jackson and Tilly Jane, two of the hottest new talents in Hollywood. They're celebrating the release of their new rom-com movie, and from what I've seen so far, the rumors of them having a torrid affair are true. However, my prediction is that it won't last beyond the month, as every chance Mr. Jackson has had to come to the counter alone he's tried to hit on me. The guy has a wandering eye that has drifted to my chest way too many times. And while he has the body of a Greek god, he's way out of luck with me. Two-timing jerks are my least favorite kind of people.

Shit, here he comes again, weaving unsteadily between the high tables. At least it's me he's decided to single out for his special brand of sleaze and not one of the waitresses.

"Mr. Jackson, how can I help you?"

"Ah, sweet Charli, you most certainly can help me. I have a big, hard problem that needs your gentle touch."

I want to roll my eyes at his not-so-subtle lines. "Really, I'm sure it's not as big or as hard as you imagine." My words drip sarcasm, but the stupid jerk doesn't even realize.

From behind me comes the familiar voice of Ryan. "Maybe I

could give you a hand to deal with your little problem."

Frowning, Chris takes a step backward. "No, all good," he stutters, and while I can't see Ryan's face behind me, I suspect from Chris's expression that Ryan is doing one of his growly, mean expressions.

"Great. Now can I call you a car?" Ryan asks, and my plastered-on fake smile turns into a real one. It's a question, but one that really only has one answer. Let's see how stupid the pretentious actor really is.

Chris darts a look right, then left, probably checking to make sure nobody else heard the exchange before responding. "Yes, call me a car," he demands, before spinning on his heel and walking away.

"Good choice," Ryan mutters so quietly that I'm sure only I hear it.

"No please or thank you there," I say as I turn to face Ryan.

A frown pulls his brow down low, his focus still on the retreating figure of Chris. "There never is with his type." He lowers his gaze to me. "Are you okay?"

"I'm fine, Ryan. You know I can take care of myself."

"I do. But still, you shouldn't have to deal with assholes like that. That's not how I run my club."

"And I appreciate that, more than you know."

Out of the corner of my eye, I spot another customer approaching, and I turn to serve them. By the time I've finished making their cocktails, Ryan has disappeared again. He has a habit of doing that. Showing up, saying a few words to me, then disappearing just as quickly. He does it at least once every shift. I wondered if it was just something he does with everyone, but when I subtly asked one of the other bartenders, they said they go weeks without seeing him. I didn't know what to make of that, so now I just expect him to pop up, and I think nothing of it.

It's a bit like our training sessions in the gym. We've sparred a few times now, and during those sessions, he talks to me like we're becoming friends. Sure, it's mostly about my technique, but there's always the occasional personal question. However in the club, he's different. Distant and aloof. I guess here it's his business, and he's a busy man.

The remainder of the night passes quietly once Chris, Tilly, and their entourage leave. I close everything down, then head down to help Tony. The colorful crowd that filled the dance floor with their erotic moves earlier has all but disappeared, probably off home, as it's nearly closing time.

Tony is busy stacking glasses when I pull myself onto a barstool. "Do you need some help?"

He smiles. "If you can hand me those last few glasses, I'll be done."

Leaning over the counter, I pass him the last of the dirty glasses. "Busy night?" I ask. Tony and I have become good friends while working closely together, and I could do with some of his lighthearted humor after the night I've had.

"Yes, surprisingly so for a Thursday night. Maybe it's the heat wave we've been having that has people a little more worked up and needing to let loose." His suggestion makes me smile.

"That must be it. Although, there must be something wrong with me if my way of unwinding is to go for a swim or run in the gym. It certainly isn't an orgy."

He laughs. "You know, an orgy isn't my go-to option either. Hey, I heard you had to deal with an asshole VIP."

"Argh. He was throwing out some of the worst pickup lines I'd ever heard, all while his celebrity girlfriend was sitting right on the other side of the room. I don't know what he thought I was going to do, duck under the table and give him a blowjob or something? He's probably seen too many bad pornos." I lean forward, resting my elbows on the just-cleaned surface. "Anyway, Ryan stepped in and suggested he leave."

"Really, that's interesting. He's never had to do that before."

I shrug, then pull out my cell to order an Uber. It's late, and I'm beat. "Anyway, my Uber is nearly here, so I'm off. I'll see you tomorrow."

Picking up my tote, I leave, and when I'm stepping from the front stone steps to the sidewalk, tracking the Uber on my cell, it cancels. *What the heck?* I hate it when that happens.

I'm so wrapped up in squinting down at the screen that I don't notice the figure standing in the shadows on the street until he speaks.

"Hi, Charli. Did you miss me?"

"What the fuck are you doing here, Brad?"

"I came to see you, of course. We've got unfinished business." The tone of his voice holds enough threat that I take a step back.

Since I stopped working at Lost Paradise, Brad has texted me a few times, but each time, I deleted the message. And the last time his message came through, I deleted him from my contacts.

"Our business was definitely finished when I left Lost Paradise." I pretend a bravado that I'm far from feeling. My hands are shaking hard as I slip my cell into my tote and drop the bag from my shoulder until I'm holding it tightly in front of me.

"It's over when I say it's over," he throws back at me through gritted teeth. Beads of sweat coat his creased forehead.

He takes two steps closer, and this time, I hold my ground. Instinctively, I know he's not here to talk. I was foolish to think the humiliation I handed him on my last night would go unpunished. He's a bully, but he kept it well hidden during the short time we were dating.

Fight or flee runs through my head like a freight train. He's too close for me to make it back to the safety of the club.

Fight it is. I widen my stance slightly. Thank God I never told him about my martial arts training, so the element of surprise is to my advantage. He has no idea what I'm truly capable of when pushed.

He takes one, then two steps closer. He can touch me now, and I prepare to drop my tote, which still hangs between us, a useless shield against whatever he plans on doing next.

"I'm warning you, Brad. Don't come any closer."

"Or what?" he sneers, the mouth that I once foolishly kissed twisted and spewing hate.

And then he makes his biggest mistake.

He grabs for my wrist.

TEN

Ryan

My new favorite pastime has become watching Charli work—especially when she smiles while making one of her special cocktails. Although grappling with her on the mats may be fast taking over the top spot. We've had three training sessions now, and if I take a cold shower before each one, I'm able to keep my dick under control.

Mostly.

I'm also not avoiding her anymore. If anything, I'm spending more time strolling around the club than I ever have in the past. Always seeking her out to catch a flirty flick of her ponytail or hear her tinkling laughter as she shares a joke with one of her colleagues.

Thankfully, the sexy little distraction left a few minutes ago after chatting to Tony, and I'm able to concentrate on what I should have already done. There was no chance of that happening while she sat on the barstool, one long leg draped over the other, a sexy-booted foot swinging. I click my computer screens to display a series of camera angles inside the club, which I do at the end of every night. There have been instances of members falling asleep in one of the rooms. But tonight there are only a few staff remaining. Moving on, I click on the exterior cameras to make sure everything is kosher, but I pause when unexpected movement catches my eye.

Who the fuck is that? I know the woman is Charli—I'd recognize her figure anywhere. But the hair on the back of my neck stands on end as I assess the situation. Something isn't right. Her stance looks like ... *Fuck!*

I'm flying out of my chair and running to the stairs at the end of the hall before I can even take a breath. After taking them two at a time, I'm down the three flights in minutes. Hoping those minutes haven't been costly for Charli. I burst out the front door like it was paper thin, not large solid wood.

And suddenly, I'm stopped in my tracks. There in front of me is Charli on the ground.

But the suspicious guy I saw moments ago is now beneath her, screaming like a two-year-old having a tantrum. Her body pins his torso to the pavement, his arm locked expertly between her thighs—the reason for his painful cries.

Not wanting to distract her, I slow my movements as I descend the stone steps to stand beside them on the sidewalk.

"Do you need any help?" I ask calmly.

"Yes, help me," the guy whines. "This crazy woman attacked me."

Charli tightens the hold imperceptibly, drawing another whimper from him.

"I wasn't speaking to you, fucker. I was asking the lady."

Charli doesn't answer or release the hold. Her only movement is the rise and fall of her shoulders as she sucks in deep breaths. I take a step closer and place my hand on her shoulder. "Charli, I can take it from here."

She looks up, her eyes dark pools filled with fear.

Now I want to hurt the fucker.

Break every bone in his hand for daring to touch her.

Smash my fist into his whimpering fucking face.

But then something else paints her expression as our gazes connect. She needs me to take control.

I loosen her hand from his wrist and help her up. "Wait over there while I have a chat with this asshole." I keep my voice low and steady, my face neutral. It's a thin mask to hide the churning violence in my gut.

Charli pulls back her shoulders, then drops her gaze to the guy still on the ground.

"Brad. The dickhead's name is Brad. He's having trouble understanding that I never want to see him again." Her words are edged with anger, slicing through the silent, dark night.

My eyebrows shoot high. She knows him. This wasn't some random assault.

"Well, maybe I can make that a little clearer." I bend down and grab the guy by the front of his sweater and pull him up. I'm considerably bigger compared to the lean pretty boy.

A flicker of fear flashes across his face when I drag him closer. "You heard her. She never wants to see you again. And if I hear you've ignored that request, then I'll find you. And it won't only be a sore shoulder you'll walk away with." I lean down closer, getting right in his face. "I'll fucking rip it from its socket. Tonight was a bad idea. Learn from it." I release him with a push, and he stumbles back. "Now get out of my face … Brad."

He swiftly walks away, and I watch him until he reaches the end of the block. Good choice.

Turning around, I find Charli sitting on the top stone step. Her head is bent over her knees, her face buried in her palms. It's like she's curled up into a small ball. I always suspected that the toughness she showed in training was a thin, fragile veneer over the vulnerability that hides under the surface. Something in her past put that fear in her, and I wonder if it's the mean bastard who just scuttled down the street like one of the city's subway rats.

I sit down beside her, leaving a couple of inches between us. "Are you okay?" Again, I work hard to keep my voice calm. The last thing she needs is me losing my shit in an unholy war of revenge.

She tilts her head to the side and peers up at me, her dark eyes filled with unshed tears. I want to scoop her into my arms. Make everything right again. Make her smile transform her features like the sun coming up at the start of the day. But I don't know that I can. Instinctively, I know this goes deeper than what just happened. I've enough experience with trauma to know there is a whole lot more going on here.

I take one of her cold, shaky hands and cover it with the warmth of mine. Then, standing one step below, I coax her up. She doesn't resist. "Come on, let me take you back inside."

Panic flashes across her face, but her voice holds some of the strength I've become accustomed to hearing from her as she blurts out, "No. I don't want anyone else to see me like this."

"Okay." My thoughts scramble as I try to come up with an alternative. "How about my place? It's above the club, and we can go directly there from the lobby."

She nods, a bunch of brown hair that came undone from her ponytail during the scuffle falling across her face, and I want to reach out and smooth it back behind her ear. But she still seems skittish, so I keep a distance between us as I lead her through the lobby to the elevator and swipe my card to take us up to the fourth floor.

It feels strange taking a woman into my private domain, even in these circumstances. When I want to spend time with a woman, it's in the club, or we go back to her place, though those occasions are rare. They never step foot in my apartment.

Silence stretches between us as Charli stands beside me, one arm wrapped around her waist, and the other gripping the straps of her tote so tightly that her knuckles appear a ghostly white.

In the elevator I quickly send Tony a text, asking him to lock up the club for me. And when the doors open directly into my apartment, I guide her out with a gentle hand on the small of her back.

"Would you like a glass of water or something stronger?" I ask, as she walks into the living room and I detour to the kitchen.

Her eyelids flutter shut and are slow to reopen, almost as though she needs a moment to process my question. "What do you have that's stronger?"

"Scotch Whiskey. And it's the good stuff."

A small smile lifts the corners of her mouth. "Whiskey it is, but only because you said it was a good one."

I pour two glasses from the bottle of Macallan Ruby single malt whiskey. Hunter gave me the bottle last Christmas, and it's still three-quarters full, as I save this one for special occasions. Tonight might not be special in the celebratory sense, but I think it's what Charli needs.

When I return to her with our drinks, she's standing statue still at the window, staring down to the street below. Both arms are now wrapped tightly around her waist, and her tote is puddled at her feet, a sweater spilling out of it. I want to hold her to make her feel safe again, but I don't think that's what she wants from me.

Instead, I ask, "Who is he?"

"A guy I dated, though not for long. But someone I should have had nothing to do with."

"He's gone now, and he won't be coming back. I'll make sure of that." I hold the glass out, and her long fingers curl around the crystal as she brings it to her lips. She takes a sip, and her lids slowly close once again.

Then, turning to me, she says, "I wish I could believe that. But they always come back."

A frown creases my forehead. "What do you mean by 'they always come back'?"

She raises the glass to her lips again, and this time, she drains it. "Brad is not the first jerk to try to force me … to do something I didn't want to do." She shudders.

"Who else did? Because I swear I'll make them regret it."

Her attempt to smile falls short. "It was a long time ago." She turns and walks over to my navy sofa and sits. I detour to the kitchen to grab the bottle of whiskey before refilling our glasses and taking a seat beside her.

"Will you tell me about it?"

The shrug of her shoulders is another attempt by her to brush off the conversation as not important, but I don't buy it. I've always been good at reading people's expressions and actions, not just their words. This conversation is a big deal to her.

"I grew up in a small town north of Sydney with Tori—my twin sister—and Jane. Jane is my mother, but she never liked us calling her Mum, so we didn't. It was also pretty clear to us that she didn't want to act like a mother, either. There was a constant stream of men filing through our house. I still don't know if they paid for the privilege or if they really were her boyfriends like she told us. When we were sixteen, one of the so-called boyfriends decided that Jane was a little too old for his tastes, and that my sister and I were much more appealing."

My fists clench and I hold my breath, fearing what comes next. She shrugs her shoulders and takes another long swallow of her drink. "He approached my bed first, and even though I had won medals in Brazilian jiu-jitsu, I froze." She tilts her head to look at me. "Luckily, my sister had heard him come in and was on his back before he could really even do anything. We took him down together and screamed for help. Jane came, chucked him out, and promised to never bring her friends back to the house again. Of course, that only lasted six months, and by that time, Tori and I had turned seventeen and saved up enough money to move to Sydney."

My stomach roils at the thought of what could have happened. If there was a chance that I could find that guy, he wouldn't be able to walk into another young girl's room.

"You fought back tonight when Brad tried to attack you."

Her pretty lips part on a soft breath. "Yes, I did. Didn't I?" The question is asked like she's afraid that it might not be true.

"Charli, you handled the situation perfectly this time." It's the truth. She's just having trouble accepting it.

"Thank you," she whispers, then places her hand on my arm.

The touch of her fingers against my skin has me imagining how good her small hand would feel on other parts of my body. And I'm an asshole for thinking this. Now is *not* the time.

I clear my throat and change the subject in an attempt to distract her. "Tell me more about your twin sister. I can't believe there are two of you." I knew she had a twin, and I've discovered a few other things about her when we've talked during our training sessions.

With a deep exhale, she leans back against the cushions, looking more relaxed since she entered my apartment. "Double the trouble—that's what all the teachers used to say about us. Except for one teacher in year six, Miss Robins, who took us under her wing." She chuckles. "Did you see what I did there?"

A laugh rumbles up from my chest. "I did get that." I'm glad her quirky sense of humor is making a reappearance, even if it's probably due to the two glasses of whiskey she just drank rather than anything I've said.

"Tell me, why was Miss Robins special?" I offer her another refill, and she nods. This will have to be the last one before I order her an Uber to take her home.

She twists her whole body to face me and hooks one leg up underneath. "Well, she was the one who introduced my sister and me to martial arts." Her brow wrinkles cutely. "Looking back as an adult, I think she could see there were going to be problems for us in the future. Jane's lifestyle was well-known in the area. You could say we were not only from the wrong side of the tracks but from crooked ones as well."

"If it makes you feel any better, my side of the tracks had some serious kinks in it too." I don't know why I just admitted that to Charli. This isn't about me; it's about helping her. I take a big gulp from my glass, hoping the revelations about my own past stay locked away.

"I've heard about your kinks," she says, and the mouthful of whiskey I was in the process of swallowing nearly comes straight back out again. Instead, it goes down about as smoothly as the moonshine my grandpa used to make in the back shed, leaving me coughing and spluttering.

A cheeky grin lights up Charli's whole face, and she reaches out to pat me on the back. "Are you alright?"

"Fine," I croak out. It's a lie, of course, because I want to find whoever it was who's been telling Charli about my kinks and make sure they never discuss my personal life again. "What exactly have you heard?"

The hand she used to pat my back slides up to rest on my shoulder.

"I heard you like to play with ropes." Her voice has become breathless, and the sound of it sends a rush of blood south. "I think I'd like to try that." Her fingers inch across to the back of my neck, and she trails her long nails along the strip of bare skin between my hair and collar. Fuck, it feels amazing.

Now that I can swallow again, I smile back at her and lean my head closer. "Maybe I can show you?"

She places her still-full glass on the coffee table in front of her. "And will you show me the rest of the private playrooms? I've been wondering if that's where you do your rope thing."

A grin spreads across my face. "First, it's not a rope thing. It's called Shibari, which is an ancient form of Japanese rope bondage. And yes, sometimes I've used the private playrooms, but sometimes not."

"What, like here?"

"No, never here."

"Why?"

"Because I never bring women here."

"Yet I'm here." She's right, of course. And strangely, it doesn't bother me that she is. "Oh yeah, but that was only because I had a breakdown."

"Maybe this time it was. But I might have brought you here anyway."

Our eyes meet briefly, and in that moment, a flurry of unspoken words seems to pass between us.

It's time I admitted the truth. "I'd love to wrap your gorgeous body in my silk ropes, Charli. You just need to ask."

"I know," she admits, her confidence firmly back in place.

I guess I haven't been very good at hiding my desire. But her intriguing mix of self-confidence and vulnerability captured my interest from that first day when she ran into me.

Her fingers continue to scratch through my short hair, and I reach out to tuck a stray strand of hers behind her ear. She leans into my touch, and her palm flattens against the back of my head, pulling me to her.

Our lips touch gently at first, learning the feel of our mouths coming together for the first time before I run the tip of my tongue along the pillowy softness of her bottom lip, and she opens to me on a soft gasp.

She tastes so fucking sweet, there's no chance I'll have the strength of will to stop us from making a monumental mistake.

ELEVEN

Charli

Ryan traces a path across my bottom lip with his tongue, each lazy stroke pressing harder. His touch is as perfect as I imagined it to be.

Our lips meld like they always belonged together. His breath becoming mine, and mine his.

The kiss deepens, turning firm and needy, and he reaches up to cup my jaw. My hand grips tighter to the back of his head. It's too late to stop now, and I won't let him.

The dam broke with his admission that he wants me in his ropes. Heat warms my body and fuels my passion for this man. I want everything he can give me and more.

He releases my mouth, pressing his forehead to mine. "I fucking want you."

"And I fucking want you to have me." There should be no doubt in his mind that I'm completely on board with us doing some serious fuckery.

He leans me back onto the sofa, and I hold tight to the nape of his neck. He follows me down, but not fully, bracing himself above me. His corded, muscular arms hold his chest above me, while from our hips down, our bodies are fused together. His erection presses into my thigh, more impressive than when I felt him in our first training session, and my heart rate picks up.

"Lose the top," he growls, and I shimmy the camisole up, stopping just beneath my breasts. His electric-blue gaze feasts on my bared stomach.

He sucks in a breath. "You like teasing me, don't you?"

The smile I give him is the only answer he needs.

"But if you were bound, you couldn't do that. Instead, I would do the teasing." He leans down and sucks one silk-covered nipple into his mouth, rolling the pebbled peak with his tongue. Damn, his mouth is hot. He reaches a hand up between us to twist my other nipple, his fingers burning through the silk.

Everything about him is hot.

A shiver skitters up my spine as he trails kisses across the bared strip of skin, then down to my belly button. A breathy moan falling from my lips.

"Yes," I mutter as he continues his exploration, and my fingers twist in the fabric of his T-shirt. "Lose the top," I mimic his words from earlier, and it earns me a deep, throaty chuckle.

"Only when I've got you completely naked." Now, *that's* a challenge I'm willing to take if it means I can get my hands on his rock-hard abs.

Our training sessions are the closest I ever get to checking them out, but it's only ever a peek. He insisted after the first time that we wear our martial arts Gi, and only if his belt loosens have I had a glimpse beneath the fabric folds.

"You've got a deal. But first, you're going to have to hop up." I tap him on the shoulder, and he pushes himself off me to sit back on the sofa. Confusion pulls his brow low as I jump up to stand in front of him.

"Are you ready for this?" I ask in what I hope is a sexy voice.

He nods slowly, still looking a little unsure.

The whiskey has loosened my tongue and, more importantly, helped me to forget Brad and the stupid dick move he tried to pull tonight. Now Ryan is giving me the opportunity to completely erase Brad from my mind and body, and I don't care that he's my boss or that this might be a bad idea.

Honestly, in this moment, I don't care about a lot of the things that would normally stop me from being impulsive. I want him, and I know he wants me. And that's the start and end of it.

His gaze narrows on me. Then, with the flexibility of a ballet dancer, I bend deeply at the waist to remove my ankle boots. I pop the button on my jeans, slide the zipper down, and, hooking my fingers in the sides, peel them down my legs. The silk camisole and white lace G-string still cover me, but barely.

Ryan's electric-blue gaze narrows, and his Adam's apple bobs in his throat on a deep swallow. "I feel like I should have put some seductive music on, because this is one of the sexiest strip shows I've ever seen."

A strong sense of empowerment pumps heat through my veins, and I curl my fingers under the silk hem of my top. "High praise indeed from the sex club owner." I inch the fabric up from my waist, its slippery softness teasing my skin.

When the curves of my breasts are visible but the fabric still covers my areola, I stop. "Does this earn me your T-shirt?"

"Absolutely." He shrugs it off over his head and reclines against the cushions, his arms spread wide as I drink in his ripped torso. Each ab defined so perfectly that they could be carved from stone. And a tattoo, *The only easy day was yesterday*, scrawled in a beautiful script on his upper chest above them. Nice.

With the confidence of someone who knows how damn sexy he is, he drawls, "You don't get the rest until you lose that." He gestures toward my top.

I inch the camisole up and off, taking my time to drive him wild before dropping it to the floor.

With a pop of my hip, I place my hand on it. "Do you want to see more?"

"I want to fucking see and feel everything. Up close." He leans forward, his face so close that his breath fans against my skin. I ache for his touch, but he doesn't give me it. So I slide my hands from my waist, capturing the thin strip of fabric on my hips and drawing it down, revealing all of me to him.

"You're gorgeous." His gaze burns me up like bright laser beams. And if him just looking at me makes me this wet, imagine what ...

But I don't have to use my imagination, because he has dropped to his knees in front of me and is spreading my legs wide.

"Hold on," he growls, and I dig my fingers into the solid, hard muscles at his shoulders.

The second I'm holding tight, he hooks an arm under one leg and lifts it to his shoulder. When he said he wanted to see me up close, he wasn't joking. He blows a puff of warm breath against my core, and my body shakes so violently that I almost lose my footing.

"Keep holding tight," he murmurs. And my fingers dig into his skin. I have an overwhelming urge to mark him, and I've no idea where the hell that thought came from. But when he places a soft kiss on the inside of my thigh, my mind goes completely blank. No more thoughts. Just feelings.

A moan slips from my lips with one swipe of his tongue along my folds. And my bones turn liquid with another. He doesn't need ropes to hold me down. His tongue is doing an amazing job of restraining me.

"That is so fucking good," I manage to gasp out in a husky voice that I don't even recognize as my own. The words seem to encourage him to concentrate his efforts on my clit. Laving the nub, then sucking it. I want him to bury his face in my pussy and not come up for breath.

But then he nips. His bite the hot spark needed to send my control up in flames, like a lit match to dry kindling, and my body burns for more.

The intensity of every lick, suck, and nip of his teeth causes another flood of heat. I'm so damn soaked with desire.

"Oh … my … God … Please." My breathing is so choppy I can no longer form a coherent sentence. I dig my fingers deeper into his flesh, seeking a solid purchase as I tumble toward a release. And when, in one swift movement, he plunges two fingers into my channel, a gasp steals the breath from my body and my hips buck.

This is no longer a gentle seduction. It's raw, out-of-control passion. And I ride his hand like I'm a rodeo champion, my muscles clenching and his name repeating on my lips.

Then my vision grows hazy as an orgasm twists my body, my mouth dropping open in a silent scream of release.

I collapse over him and cradle his head to me. I don't think I'll ever be the same person again after that.

We stay curled together until my breathing returns to something resembling normal.

He leans back against the edge of the sofa, his smile wide and his mouth embarrassingly wet. "Now get that cute ass of yours up on the sofa so I can fuck you into tomorrow."

I didn't think I had anything left to give. But his words fire my blood up with thoughts of his cock sinking into me. Still breathing hard, I crawl over him to kneel on the sofa, my hands braced against the back.

"That is one beautiful sight," he mutters, looking up at me suspended over his face, and my knees nearly give out. But the embarrassment of falling has me stiffening my position and leaning my body weight forward to rest my forehead on the cushioned headrest.

Another of his deep, delicious chuckles rolls over me. The sound so good a shiver runs up my spine. He pulls himself to a stand, and my knees soften. Tilting my head to the side, I watch him pull a condom from his wallet and undo his jeans before pulling them and his black boxers down.

His cock bounces free, slapping against his waist.

I jerk my head up from the cushion. "Fuck, that's impressive" pops out before I can clamp my hand over my mouth.

"I'm glad you approve," he responds as he kicks his clothes and shoes away. "But what's impressive is what I can do with it."

"You talk a big game," I tease.

"I am a big game." He waggles his brows at me, and I giggle at his silly banter.

Though, I swear my pussy weeps with delight at the promised fun.

TWELVE

Ryan

Lust has never felt so fucking good. And it's nearly got me shooting my load as I squeeze the base of my pulsing cock to gain some control. Charli on all fours, fully displayed to me and still glistening from her orgasm, is a sight to behold. One I frankly never thought I'd get the chance to see. Yet here we are, and I'm not about to waste a moment.

Her taste still lingers on my tongue, making my mouth water for more, so I swipe a finger through her folds, then bring it to my mouth. *Delicious*. And her soft gasp is almost as sweet.

With my chest pressed against her back, I lift her chin to capture another one before it slips from her pretty mouth, sucking her bottom lip between my teeth. My fingers return to her pussy and plunge into her tight heat, preparing her for me. I twist them while rubbing my thumb across her clit. Already, she feels close again.

"Oh … fuck," she whimpers, and I swallow her words as she pushes back onto my fingers.

She's so eager and responsive to my touch. But it's not my fingers I want her fucking this time. Firmly, I grasp hold of my cock and rub it through her slick folds. "Are you ready to play?" I whisper close to her ear.

"Yes," is her needy reply. And with no further warning, I thrust hard and fast into her heat.

Her exultant cry is almost as fantastic as the tight grip of her walls around my cock, the squeeze narrowing my vision. Fucking amazing. I withdraw to my tip before pushing back in to the base again, and this time, her moans fill the room and her back arches high.

A whisper leaves her lips, and I lean forward to catch it.

"More," she repeats, then begins to rock up and down on my dick. The little firecracker is demanding with her needs.

Without hesitation, I wrap one hand around her ponytail and place another on her shoulder. Then, matching my pace to hers, I pump into her sweet body, our bodies finding a rhythm that's uniquely ours.

She chants my name softly at first, then louder.

Faster and faster, I pump into her like a force of nature building in intensity. Charli is a category five hurricane wreaking havoc on my control. But I need her ready to surge over the ledge with me, so I reach my hand around to her clit, rubbing it.

"Yes, yes, yes," she cries out as her walls clamp down around my cock.

"Fuck!" The word is dragged up from deep in my chest and explodes into the room as my cum fills the condom over and over.

She shudders, falling against the cushions, and I curl in tightly over her back, my arms wrapping around her waist, holding her close. I'm not ready to let go.

"Sooo ... that was pretty spectacular," she says from beneath me, and I lift up, pulling out. Already, I feel the loss.

I remove the condom, tie it off, and walk to the kitchen to dispose of it. When I turn back, she's standing next to the sofa, looking down at the pile of discarded clothes on the rug. Her brow furrowed and her lips twisted to the side like she's already beginning to question what just happened.

Before she has a chance to find the answers, I take her hand with mine. "Come with me." When she looks to be hesitating, I add, "Please."

"Okay," she whispers, and lets me lead her to my bedroom.

Every beautiful inch of Charli deserves to be worshipped—to be made mine. And that's what I plan to spend the rest of the night doing.

I want to explore every dip and curve of her gorgeous body.

Extract every thought from her beautiful mind.

And simply be right here holding her close in my arms, keeping her safe from the asshole-Brads of the world.

**

Out of habit, I wake before the alarm has a chance to do its thing. What's surprising this morning, after only a couple hours of sleep, is that for once, I'm not in one of my bad moods.

Honestly, losing sleep with Charli in my bed is something I could get used to. It was a night to remember.

Before I've even opened my eyes, I reach for her warm body. But my hand finds nothing except a bundle of empty, rumpled sheets on the other side of my bed.

What the fuck?

Blinking the sleep from my eyes doesn't change the reality.

She's not there. But when I lift my head, I find her fully dressed, all the way down to her boots, and sitting in the chair in the corner of my room.

"Good morning," she says calmly. But I'm not fooled by her casual greeting. I sense there isn't going to be anything good about this morning. She sits stiffly in the chair, one hand gripping the armrest and the other twisting the strap on the bag in her lap.

What happened to the woman who, only a few hours ago, was in my arms, begging for more? Who moaned, whimpered, and cried out my name through each of her three orgasms. And then fell into an exhausted sleep curled against my chest.

Only once I'm propped up against the headboard do I speak. "What are you doing all the way over there? Instead of here beside me."

"I need to go," she answers, but for some reason, she doesn't seem to be able to look me in the eye.

"Why? You don't have a shift until tonight. Where do you need to go?"

Her eyelids flutter shut like she's trying to make up some bullshit reason to give me. But when she opens them again, she bends forward, looking at the floor rather than me. "You're my boss, Ryan. We shouldn't have done this." Her voice is a flat monotone, rather than the sunshiny cheerfulness I've become used to.

"Don't you think it's a little late to be saying that?" I'm not going to let her get away with regrets. What we did last night was fucking amazing.

"Yes. But not too late to stop us from doing it again. The whole mess with Brad happened because we worked together."

"Don't compare me to that asshole," I snarl, regretting my tone instantly when she jumps.

"Sorry. I wasn't. I only meant the situation, not the person." She twists one strap around her finger. "I love working at the club, and

I don't want to leave. But that's what will have to happen if this all blows up in our faces."

She's right. She's got more to lose than me. Disappointment feels like a gut punch.

"I get it," I admit as I rub a hand across my bare chest, trying to ease the tightness. "But don't expect me to regret it for one second."

She stands and walks toward the bedroom door. When she reaches it, she looks back over her shoulder, our gazes locking for the first time today as she says, "I don't regret it either."

Then she turns and leaves. And the worst part ... I let her.

THIRTEEN
Charli

"What time do you call this?" Sadie asks when I poke my head around the corner of the doorway. She's leaning against the kitchen counter, drinking a mug of coffee and grinning from ear to ear.

With a huff, I drop my bag to the floor. "Coffee time?" The strong, bitter aroma of freshly ground beans wafts across the narrow space, and I almost want to snatch the mug from her hands. "Or it could be time I grew up and stopped making bad choices when it comes to men."

"Okayyy. This sounds interesting. Sit, girl, and let me get you that coffee." Sadie zips around our tiny kitchen like she's hit fast-forward, making me a coffee and magicking up some flaky pastries from a cupboard.

My brow crinkles. "Are those fresh?"

Hands on her hips, she spins to a stop. "Yes … well, fresh enough. I got them from work yesterday." Sadie working at a local French patisserie is the best.

"They look good." My mouth waters in anticipation of the first bite. Last night's dinner at the club was more a quick snack than anything of real substance. I had planned to eat something when I got home from my shift, but that all changed after running into Brad.

Sadie places the plate in front of me with a clunk, and a couple of toasted almond flakes topple from the pastry. I pick one up and pop it in my mouth while I wait for her to settle on the stool beside me.

"Right. Now, before we start, do we need to get Tori on FaceTime?"

I check my cell. Tori sent a message a little earlier saying she was boarding her flight to London. "We can't. She's on her flight already." Quickly, I send her a text, asking if she can call me when she arrives at her friend's place. She'll be staying in London for a few days before flying to New York.

I place my cell face down on the counter and bring my mug to my lips, breathing the rich steam in deeply before taking a sip. This first coffee of the day, with my favorite freshly ground beans, is always the best.

Sadie watches me closely, and when I place the mug back on the counter, she asks, "Are you ready to tell me what happened?"

All of the energy that had me fleeing Ryan's apartment as if a pack of rabid dogs were chasing me seeps from my bones. I'm annoyed at myself for repeating the mistakes of the past by fooling around with someone I work with. And it's worse this time. He's my *boss*. My totally hot, best-sex-ever boss.

"I think I've fucked up," I state bluntly. It's the honest truth, and as the coffee works its magic, warming my cold, shaky limbs, I explain exactly how.

I start by telling her how Brad cornered me on the sidewalk outside work. She listens silently as I replay the conversation, only interjecting occasionally with the same repeated word: *Asshole*. The words I have for him are a lot stronger when it comes to that sick fucker. When I get to the part where he grabbed my wrist and pulled me toward him, she jumps up from her stool and wraps me in a hug.

"Oh my God. Please tell me you kicked his butt."

I smile, something I didn't think I'd be able to do remembering the moment. All those years of training and competition, when I was left bruised and hurting by my stronger opponents, finally feel worth it.

"I did kick his butt. In fact, I laid his nasty arse out flat on the sidewalk." Thinking about that moment now, I'm damn proud of myself, though at the time, I was scared to death. Scared that I would freeze. Scared I would forget everything I'd learned about how to protect myself.

"It was horrible," I whisper from within the tight hold of Sadie's hug. She may be smaller than me, but she gives a fierce hug, and I've needed a few of those over the months we've lived together.

"Oh, Charli." Her voice is soft like a warm wool blanket tucking around me.

"It's okay. I'll be okay." I say the words more to reassure myself than Sadie. It seems to work for both of us, as she loosens her hold on me and drops onto the stool behind her.

Settled back at the counter, she picks up her coffee, and I'm glad to have the moment to gather my thoughts before continuing.

"Lucky for me, Ryan appeared beside me and dealt with Brad."

I'm still confused by Ryan showing up like he did, but I'm grateful. I've no idea what I would have done next if he hadn't. Sure,

I had the bastard secured, so he couldn't hurt me, but that didn't really leave me any option to call someone for help.

"Ryan, your boss?" Sadie asks before taking a bite of her pastry. I've mentioned Ryan to her before now, but no more than what I've said about Tony or any of the other people I work with at the club.

She certainly has no idea of the extent to which he takes up space in my thoughts. I haven't even spoken about him much with Tori.

"Yes, my boss. The guy I spar with occasionally." I turn my head to the side to look at her, and I wish I hadn't. She's squinting at me like I've got a secret, and she's determined to get it out of me.

She pushes her empty plate away and spins on the stool to face me, then crosses her arms over her chest. "Tell me again about Ryan, your boss?"

A sigh slips from my lips. "Fine. I like him. He's hot in a rough, mountain-man kind of way. All broad shoulders, ripped abs, and thick, muscled thighs like he spends his days chopping down trees with a hand saw." The description of his body flows from my lips like a piece of memorized poetry. Now that I have intimate knowledge of his body, I could probably go on and on about every glorious inch of him. Ryan is poetry in motion.

"And when, exactly, did you get to see his ripped abs?" Sadie asks, a grin stretching her mouth wide.

"Well, after the Brad incident, Ryan took me up to his apartment. It's above the club and ... we kind of got naked." I squeeze my eyes shut, waiting for her reaction. And when it comes, it's not the shocked reprimand I expect.

She giggles. "How do you 'kind of' get naked? What, you walked in the door, and the air con was up so high that your clothes blew off? Or the air con wasn't working, and it was so hot that you had to strip?"

"Stop," I beg, laughing so hard that my sides hurt. "We had a drink. We talked a little. One thing led to another, we got naked, and then we had sex."

"Whoa, girl. You are leaving out so many juicy details."

For reasons I'm not willing to think too hard about, I don't feel like sharing all the juicy details about my night with Ryan. He's different, and I want to keep the moments we shared to myself. So I can remember them one by one in the privacy of my room when I finally drag my tired body to bed.

"He was amazing, helping me deal with the emotional aftermath of Brad. As I said before, I like him, and I've noticed that he likes me. We were sitting on his sofa talking, and then we kissed." My lids lower to half-closed at the memory of his touch, his body.

When I raise them again, Sadie is staring at me wide-eyed. "He was that good?"

"Everything about him was spectacular. But he's my boss. I swore I wouldn't get involved with someone I worked with again. Yet here I am, having done exactly that."

"How dare he be a sex god *and* be your boss," Sadie exclaims.

"Is that all you've got to say? Nothing about me being a weak, unprincipled fool?" I groan, trying to hold back the smile threatening to break across my face.

Her eyes are brimming with laughter as she stands and walks over to the coffee maker. "I'll leave that to you to beat yourself up over. Do you want another coffee?"

"Yes, please. And do we have any more of those pastries? If I'm going to be beating myself up over my night of hot sex, I'll need more sustenance."

I watch her make our coffees and grab another two pastries from a secret stash she seems to have hidden in the cupboard. And while she's doing all that, my swirling thoughts about Ryan are beginning to coalesce into the unhappy conclusion that I shouldn't have left so quickly this morning. We should have talked more about what had happened.

Sadie returns to the counter with two fresh mugs of coffee. "Look ... I don't get it. You've had a night of hot sex with a hot guy, and that's fantastic. I'd be shouting it from the rooftops. No, hold on." She holds her hand up, and I wait for her to continue. "You know what I'd be doing. I'd still be in his bed, getting myself some more of that hot sex."

"Argh! You think I should have stayed." I wanted to stay too. That's why I sat in the chair for half an hour watching him sleep. The first time I'd truly seen him looking relaxed. No frown lines across his forehead. No scowl pulling the corners of his mouth down. And his icy-blue eyes, for once, not drilling into my soul.

"Of course you should have stayed," she confirms, settling back on her stool. "From what you've told me, Ryan is nothing like Brad."

No! He was there when I needed him. There when I broke down afterward. Looked after me.

I probably shouldn't have slept with my boss, but I did. And it wasn't because I'd had too much alcohol, or because Brad threatened me. Ryan and I were inevitable from the first day we met.

"Damn! I owe him an apology. I shouldn't have left like I did. It was a bitchy thing to do."

My declaration is met with silence from Sadie. She obviously agrees.

***

Another shift is nearly finished, and again, I haven't seen Ryan. He's obviously avoiding me.

I know I shouldn't be surprised after the way I left things the other morning, but seriously, the longer he hides, the more awkward it will be when we do have to face each other.

I want to apologize to him in person, but that would rely on him being physically here.

"Tony, is Ryan away? I haven't seen him around lately." I never wanted to have to ask Tony, but he's the only person who'd know.

"No, he's not away. Just holed up in his office. I wouldn't recommend disturbing him unless it was really important. He's like a hungry grizzly bear that just woke up from winter hibernation. Fucking angry."

He finishes polishing the glass with the soft cloth in his hands, making sure it's streak-free. It's a shared pet peeve. You can't make a pretty cocktail in a smudgy glass.

"Is it anything I can help with?" he asks.

"Not really. Do you mind if I take my break now?"

"No, go. But don't say I didn't warn you." He picks up the next glass and starts the polishing process again.

Great. As if I wasn't nervous enough apologizing to Ryan, now I've got Tony's warning playing on repeat in my head as I climb the stairs to the third floor.

FOURTEEN

Ryan

A soft knock raps on the door, and I growl, "Come in." Even here in my office, my supposed sanctuary, I can't escape.

The door opens slowly, and the one person I didn't expect to see peeps her head around the corner. "Does the invitation to come in still stand if it's me?" Charli asks.

I know I've been a complete asshole lately. Earlier, I even chewed out one of the new waitresses for dropping a glass, something I've never done before. Any moron could have seen it wasn't her fault. With the crowd, it's almost impossible for them to move around with trays full of cocktails. Generally, my staff like me, and I don't like Charli thinking she can't speak to me.

"Sure. Take a seat." I gesture toward one of the black leather visitor's chairs on the other side of my desk.

She moves to follow my command, her head held high and her back ramrod straight. Today's outfit is a zip-up leather crop top with black Lycra leggings. It's new, and with the zipper halfway down, her irresistibly deep cleavage is on full display. I lose the battle to keep my eyes above her neck. It's impossible when I now know how beautiful those tits are. How perfectly they fill my hands. And how sensitive they are to my touch.

The memory pisses me off. I drag my eyes away and then stand, coming around my desk to sit on the edge facing her.

Arms folded across my chest, I ask, "Do you want something?" If I'm honest, I'm hoping she'll admit that she wants me. But I know that's a complete long shot after the way we left things.

Her eyes dart up to mine but don't rest there for long, quickly dropping down again to stare at a spot in the middle of my chest. Maybe she can see my heart beating beneath the thin fabric. It's pumping so fast against my chest wall that it wouldn't be surprising to find that it was visible.

"Actually, I do. I want to talk to you."

I wait for her to continue, and when she shuffles her feet into a supposedly more comfortable position, she does. "Are you avoiding me?"

I've become accustomed to Charli coming straight out and saying what's going on in her beautiful head. In that way, she's refreshingly different from any other woman I've been attracted to. Her openness deserves the same honesty. "Based on our last conversation, that's what I thought you wanted."

"No. Not at all. I've been looking for you."

"Really? I'm not hard to find." I unlock my arms from my chest and spread them wide, proving my point. "But why?" My eyes narrow, wishing she would look up at me.

I get my wish when her dark gaze flicks up, scorching me like a pair of flame throwers. "You know, you can be an arsehole sometimes."

I choke out a laugh. "Is that how you should be talking to your boss?"

"It was you who told me you're my boss's boss. And honestly, when we've done the things we did the other night, then all pretense of politeness is just that ... pretense." She nearly spits the word at me.

Taking my time, I lean forward to place a hand on each armrest, trapping her beneath me. The slight catch in her breath reminding me of her gasps when I ran my tongue along her sweet folds, tracing a hot, wet path from the top down to her entrance. *Delicious.*

My voice is gruff as I admit, "I don't want you to be polite. I want you talking dirty to me. Filthy, crude words spilling from those pretty lips, like I know you're capable of."

She presses the pillowy softness of her lips together, and I smile at her reaction.

Dropping her gaze, she whispers, "Please stop. That isn't why I'm here." With her hands squeezed together on her lap and her feet flat against the floor, I'm not fooled by her calm tone.

"Again, I have to ask. Why are you here?"

She clears her throat. "I came here to apologize for running away." This time, her voice is strong and clear.

Damn, I love how she doesn't back down. Even when she's nervous like she clearly is now, she takes up my challenges. "That could be almost as good as dirty talk," I tease, unable to resist the taunt. "But you don't need to apologize."

I lift a hand to brush away that one lock of dark hair that's always coming loose from her ponytail. My finger twists through the silky strands, and more memories of me wrapping a fistful of her glossy dark hair around my hand fill my head. It's so soft as I lift it to my face and breathe in the scent of summer. I don't know if it's her perfume or shampoo, but after the other night, it's been imprinted on my pillow and in my senses.

Close to her ear, I whisper, "We both chose to cross that line, Charli." I want to ease whatever guilt she's carrying. If anyone was to blame, it was me. Taking her to my apartment, then plying her with expensive whiskey.

Her head leans in closer to mine. "Maybe it wasn't a mistake?" she says, the soft inflection at the end making it sound more of a question than a statement. But that could just be her Australian accent.

I tilt her chin up so she can't look away. "And if it wasn't a mistake, what happens next?"

Her shoulders rise and fall like she's struggling to draw in her next breath, but her silence fills the room. I want her to tell me what she wants. And fucking hope that it will be me.

"More," she confesses.

I lean back, but I'm still crowding her space. "Yes. More. That sounds like a good plan." The grin that spreads across my face would split my cheeks in half if it were any wider.

She glances down at her watch, noting the time. "I should go," she stutters, and as she stands, I push back to brace my arms on the desk's edge. If I don't hold on to the solid surface, I'll be tempted to pull her into my arms. And I won't want to stop there.

"Yes. For now." It's a promise, and the smile she gives me tells me she's recognized it as one before she turns and leaves.

The door closes with a soft snick, and I pick up my cell to call Tony.

"Hey, man. What's happening?"

I don't bother with pleasantries. "Schedule Charli in the Red Room tomorrow night."

He chuckles. "Should I ask why?"

"No."

"I guess I won't, then. Though it's interesting that when I suggested she work in that bar last week, you said no."

"I've changed my mind," I hiss through gritted teeth, then hang up before Tony can question me any further.

FIFTEEN
Charli

Exhaustion drags my shoulders down. It's quieter here, and my eyes droop as I wipe the cloth over the already sparkling marble surface. I've learned Friday nights are the busiest of the week, with the city professionals coming in to unwind from their long working hours, but in the Red Room, that doesn't equate to drink orders. These corporate types have some other interesting methods to de-stress, and I'm trying not to pay them too much attention.

An elegant woman lounges back on a nearby white leather sofa. The only thing she wears is one of the largest diamond rings I'd ever seen on her ring finger. One handsome man, probably in his early forties, is having sex with her, his ring finger adorned with a thick gold band. A younger man stands at her head, feeding her his cock, and a third fondles her breasts with one hand, while his other rubs up and down the leg of the man standing. That's wild.

The woman and her men seem totally uninhibited, completely immersed in each other. It's a struggle, but I force myself to look away, feeling like an intruder, which is utterly ridiculous because they are in an orgy room. They *want* people to see them.

This room is not what I expected. Or rather, my reaction to the scene is not what I expected. It's not my thing, but I also don't judge their choices. This isn't the debauched sex I thought it would be. There is love between these groups of people.

"Do you wish that was you?" A deep, instantly recognizable voice murmurs from behind me. The heat from his body wrapping around me like a warm embrace, though Ryan doesn't touch me physically. He doesn't have to for goose bumps to pebble my skin. My eyes close briefly, savoring this feeling, but as much as I want to, I don't lean into him.

"Well, do you?" he asks again, and this time, his tone demands a response.

"I don't think so. Not for everyone to see. Even though it looks very … freeing."

"Freeing? That's an interesting take." He stands silently behind me for a moment before saying, "I think you might be right. She's in charge of how she's being pleasured, and that would be freeing."

The woman's head drops back, and her back arches off the leather bench in the throes of orgasm.

"Fuck, that's hot," I mutter, transfixed by the scene.

"The man fucking her is her husband. He's a judge, and she's a top broker on Wall Street."

My jaw drops.

"Does that surprise you?"

"A little. And the two men?"

"They are their guests, so I don't know. Probably city suits."

Ryan's large hand curls around my hip, his fingers digging into the soft flesh as he steps in closer, trapping me between his body and the marble-top counter. There's no gap between our bodies, and his hard cock presses against the small of my back.

"I bet your pussy is dripping right now," he whispers close to my ear. "Do you want me to ease the ache? I could do that for you." His deep voice sends a shiver skittering up my spine.

A needy, soft moan slips from my lips. I'm so turned on that at this point, I'd let him do anything he wants to me. I don't care that I'm supposed to be working or that I'm in a room full of people. Granted, nobody in this room is paying any attention to me, as they're too busy fucking each other.

"How?" I whisper, completely lost in his words.

He slides his hand down the side of my Lycra leggings, then back up, hooking a thumb into the waistband. "Like this?" He peels the fabric down, inching closer to my bare pussy. "Nobody would know. They can't see what I'm doing behind the bar. And no cameras are pointed here."

"Yes. Yes, I want that." My heart is pounding so hard that there doesn't seem to be any space left for me to catch my breath.

"Place your hands on the counter and open your legs for me."

I do as he commands, gripping the cold stone edge tightly and widening my stance.

"Good girl." The words rumble up from his chest, making me ache for more.

His hand dips deeper into my leggings until he's able to run one finger through my soaked folds. Already, I feel close. My eyes squeeze shut as I try to control the increasing need to let go like the woman. But unlike her, I don't need three men to give me pleasure; only one—Ryan.

Drawing his thumb in tiny circles over my clit, he nearly brings me to my knees. My fingers spread wider on the counter.

"Open your eyes, Charli," he whispers, and I blink them open. "What do you see?"

"Fucking. Lots of fucking." My voice is husky with need. All around the dimly lit room, twenty or so people are performing sexual acts. Couples, threesomes, or more like the woman, who is now on all fours, her mouth wrapped around one guy's cock, while another pumps into her, and the third lies to the side, sucking on her tits. I need Ryan fucking me, not just teasing me.

It's like he has read my mind when he continues. "You want my cock again, don't you?"

"Yes. Yes. Yes ..." My words are lost to a loud moan as he plunges two fingers through the swollen walls of my channel, curling them up to reach that special spot, all while continuing to circle his thumb over my clit. I ride his hand. Not wildly like the other night, since someone would notice that, but with a gentle rocking. The muscles in my stomach tighten until they are like the strings on a bow stretched too far.

"I've got you," Ryan mutters in a low, deep voice that reverberates through my body—the final trigger for me to let go in an explosive but silent release.

My inner walls squeeze against his fingers until, with a shuddering breath in and out, I slump back against him.

His fingers slip from between my folds, then from my leggings, but I place my hand over his, holding his palm to my stomach.

I need a moment. My wobbly legs feel like two strands of overcooked spaghetti rather than flesh and bone that could hold me up. But one deep breath laced with my usually strong willpower and I'm straightening to stand unaided.

"Come to my office when you finish tonight," Ryan demands in a deep gravelly voice against the shell of my ear, and his hand drops away from my belly. I turn to reply but he's already walking away and I'm left open-mouthed watching his retreating back.

I can't believe I just had an orgasm in a crowded room. And even more unbelievable is that Ryan was the one who gave me it.

SIXTEEN

Ryan

I wasn't sure she'd come—not until I hear the soft knock on my office door. I know it's her and this time, it's not because I've been stalking her through the cameras. I just know.

After leaving her in the Red Room with barely a goodbye, I escaped up to my apartment to pump out my release onto the white tiled floor in my waterfall shower. She was so fucking beautiful when she climaxed. Her inner muscles squeezing against my fingers so firmly that they tingled with the loss of blood flow to them. I nearly came in my boxer briefs and that's never happened before, so instead of checking to see if she was okay, I ran.

Another soft rap against the wood has me striding over to the door, swinging it open.

Her eyes pop wide in surprise at the sudden movement, but only momentarily given the way she says a breathy, "Ryan."

My name on her lips never fails to make my cock twitch in response, even when it's said with a hint of accusation. I expect she wasn't happy with my abrupt departure.

"Please come in," I offer, stepping back to let her pass.

The hesitation in her step is only perceptible to someone like me who has made watching her an obsession. Her pupils are huge and a pretty pink flush colors her cheeks. She looks to still be feeling the aftereffects of her earlier orgasm. Well, that makes two of us.

I close the door behind her and lock it with a definitive click then twist the dimmer light switch to low. She doesn't turn from where she's stopped in the center of the room; instead, her gaze remains focused on the red silk ropes coiled on the corner of my desk.

Fuck, I hadn't meant for her to see them tonight, but earlier I'd been practicing knots as a form of stress relief. It works better for me than squeezing a rubber ball. I was so distracted when she knocked that I forgot to tuck them back into the bottom drawer.

When I'm standing close behind her, she tilts her head to the side, exposing the long column of her neck, and I want to kiss my way down the smooth skin to her collarbone. But not yet.

"Are those your ropes?" she finally asks when the silence has dragged on too long.

"Yes, those are silk Shibari ropes," I answer simply, letting her lead the conversation.

She seemed intrigued when the topic of Shibari came up that night in my apartment but that doesn't mean she wants me to bind her. It's a kink that both participants need to be into.

"How do you use them?" she asks, surprising me with the question.

"Do you want me to show you?" My breath catches in my chest, waiting for her response.

"Yes," she says, raising her chin, and the air I was holding whooshes from my lungs.

Fuck, I never expected this. Maybe I'd hoped that one day she'd agree to try some rope play, but it felt like such a slim possibility to me that she'd be into it in the same way I am.

My office suddenly feels too hot, and I run my sweaty palms down the sides of my dress pants, hoping she doesn't recognize it for what it is—nerves. I need to do this right.

"Take off your clothes," I demand in a voice more gruff than I intended.

"You do it," she responds with a tone matching the strength of mine.

"Always challenging me, sweet, innocent Charli."

"I thought we'd already established I'm not so innocent."

"True, not entirely innocent." I can't resist the urge to touch her now, and I kiss a path along her exposed neck, the same trail my eyes tracked earlier. She gasps, and the soft sound settles the nerves playing tug-a-war in my gut.

"So responsive," I murmur almost to myself.

I lift the black silk camisole over her head, then peel the stretchy Lycra from her legs. Crouching down, I lift first one foot, then the other, to remove her shoes along with the leggings. My palms tingle with desire. I want to touch every inch of her fair skin not covered by the black lacy G-string and run my hands from her ankles up over each delicious, toned curve.

With featherlight fingers, I start tracing a path up her calves, to the back of her thighs, over her bare butt cheeks before dipping my thumbs into the cute dimples just above them. It's a journey of discovery I've not yet had the opportunity to take and it can't be rushed.

My palms flatten when I reach the firm muscles of her back,

and I fan them out to her sides and around to cup her breasts. Her shoulders drop on a sigh that's half exhale and half moan. I sprinkle kisses across her shoulders as I gently massage her soft flesh. I could easily spend the next hour lavishing praise upon them, but not tonight. Tonight is about new emotional experiences.

"You really want me to bind you?" I ask again, still struggling to believe she agreed.

"Yes, please," she replies, sounding unusually compliant. Charli wants to feel my ropes around her.

My gut clenches in anticipation as I drop my hands and move around to stand in front of her.

"So very sweet," I murmur before dropping my gaze to the gorgeous tits I was just cradling. They're going to look even more beautiful bound with red silk.

"What do I do?" she asks, looking up at me with huge dark-chocolate eyes, like I hold all the answers, and my chest swells at the trust she's placing in my hands.

"Exactly what you're doing now," I reply as I undo the buttons on my white dress shirt before shrugging it off my shoulders and throwing it over the back of the nearby visitor's chair. I then stroll over to my desk and pick up the half-empty bottle of water to wet my suddenly dry throat.

Charli remains standing tall and straight, studying my every movement.

"Are you thirsty?" I offer, holding the bottle in my outstretched hand, but she shakes her head.

I gather up one of the coils from my desk and walk back to her. "Charli, I need to ask one more time. Do you want me to do this?"

"Yes, Ryan. I want you to do your Shibari thing with me." She places her hand on my forearm. "Please show me."

"Okay, but you need a safe word."

She nods, then blurts out, "Fruit salad."

My right eyebrow shoots up. "Fruit salad it is then." The words will forever be associated to this moment with this woman.

I take the end of the rope, running it through my fingers a couple of times. The softness of the silk will feel more like a caress against her skin.

"Put your arms behind your back." I try to keep my voice gentle but it comes out rough with desire.

Her pupils are huge but she does as I ask.

I move behind her again and begin to bind her hands in a basic double column tie. Her chest rises and falls with rapid breaths and leaning close, I whisper, "Relax, sweetheart. I promise you'll like this." With a shuddering deep inhale, the tension in her shoulders seems to dissolve.

Normally, I would work silently when I bind a woman, speaking only to confirm ongoing consent until I'm done. But Charli is different. She's always been different. So with each new technique or knot, I explain what I'm doing in a way that's reminiscent of our training sessions in the gym. But also very different, as each explanation is accompanied by a sprinkling of kisses along her jawline, neck, and shoulders.

She stands statue still, not speaking but her eyes sparkle with interest as she watches what I'm doing. Her head tilting to various angles so she can better see my work. I now wish we'd done this in one of the playrooms in front of a large floor-to-ceiling mirror so she could see how amazing she looks already. But honestly, my plans when I asked Charli to come to my office tonight never involved this. Fucking yes, but not Shibari.

"Do you like the way the knots feel on your skin?" I ask tenderly as I bring the excess rope around her in a tight upper chest strap.

"Yes," she murmurs, and it sounds more like a soft moan as I deliberately brush my knuckles across her pebbled nipples. Each movement is made with the intention of producing sensations that bring her pleasure. And from the sounds she's making, it seems to be working.

I love her little whimpers as I continue wrapping her body to form a lower chest strap under the swell of her breasts.

"This form of chest harness is called, the Shinju," I say as I connect the upper and lower straps together between her tits, trapping and accenting them between the blood-red strands of silk that I twist and run over her shoulders.

I've never seen a more beautiful woman than Charli in this moment. That she asked me to do this with her makes my heart race like it's trying to escape from my chest. An intensity has been building between us with each touch and knot against her smooth, soft skin, like I'm imprinting myself in the very cells of her epidermis.

The rope will leave a faint mark on her body that will fade in hours, but these strong feelings that tighten my chest almost painfully will last much longer.

I attempt to clear the sudden lump from my throat before continuing in a neutral tone that I hope masks the confused thoughts tumbling around in my head. "Each pattern is designed to stimulate your erogenous zones." My hands work efficiently to tighten the last knot.

Her only response is a barely audible gasp as her darkened brown eyes droop halfway closed in a final sigh of submission.

"Good girl," I whisper the words of praise.

She appears to be teetering on the edge. Goose bumps cover every inch of exposed smooth skin and her chest rises and falls with rapid stuttering breaths.

"Are you okay?" I ask and she nods. For this first time I don't want to overwhelm her, so I'll only restrain her upper body.

"Do you remember your safe word?" She nods again.

"Do you want to use it?" Her ponytail swings wildly behind her as she shakes her head.

The tension of the ties around her tits makes them look fuller, pushing them up and out. I dip my head to suck one taut nipple between my teeth. Charli's entire body trembles and the muscles in her restrained arms flex. This is challenging her naturally independent nature which likes to have control. I move to the other rosy bud, and she arches her back, pushing her chest forward to meet my open mouth. I suck and nip, lavishing her tits with affection until my cock is like a rod of steel, straining painfully against my pants zipper.

I kick off one shoe, then the second, sending it tumbling across the floor and landing with a thud. I retrieve the condom I placed in my pocket earlier then almost rip my pants from my body before unceremoniously throwing them away.

Charli's eyes pop wide at the sound of crinkled foil. Two large dark pools of passion lock onto mine, and in that moment, a stream of unspoken words seems to pass between us. She's close already. And, quite frankly, so am I.

"Open your legs," I demand.

When she widens her stance, I slip my finger into her G-string and run it through her soaking folds, coating it liberally before bringing it to my mouth and sucking it clean. I'd drop to my knees and feast if I thought I'd be able to do that without shooting my load. I'm only hanging by a thread, so instead, I move her closer to my desk, then snatch up my discarded shirt and bunch it in my fist, forming a makeshift pillow. With a swipe of my hand, I clear a space on the dark wood surface.

"Lean forward, angel," I tell her before easing her down with a palm between her shoulder blades. Her cheek rests on my shirt, her bound breasts still accessible, and her butt is high in the air.

With a gentle tap on her ass, I direct her to spread her legs again. The thin strip of black lace still covers her but barely. With two fingers twisted into the delicate fabric, I tear it from her body.

Another gasp leaves her lips. She's perfect.

It's only then that I free my cock from my boxer briefs and give it a firm tug before covering it, my gaze never wavering from the glorious sight of Charli bent over my desk, waiting for me to fuck her. Tightening my grip around the base of my cock, I give it a couple more tugs before placing it between her creamy thighs. With a tilt of my hips, I slide my hard rod along her soft glistening folds, coating it like I did my finger as she writhes beneath me. Her moans grow louder, not caring if anyone still in the club can hear.

"Ryan, fuck me, please," she begs, then adding more fiercely, "Just fuck me."

But I don't yet. Instead, I continue to tease her, rubbing the head of my cock around her entrance. And only when she's virtually screaming for me to fill her, do I thrust into her heat.

Her knees wobble but she remains upright mainly because my hands are on her hips for support. She pushes her body back to meet mine as I pump in and out.

Guttural incoherent sounds spill from her mouth, bouncing off the walls of my office and reverberating back to us. She's like a wild animal unleashed, and I'm not much tamer.

We fuck hard, her walls clenching around me tighter and tighter until she's literally milking the cum from my balls as she explodes with my name on her lips.

Our skin slick with sweat, I fold my body over hers, wrapping my arms around her waist. She's still restrained and I don't want her to fall.

"Are you okay?" I ask for the second time tonight, concern pulling my brow low. "I'm sorry that was out of control."

She lifts her head slightly. "Are you crazy? That was the best orgasm ever." Her voice sounds a little shaky in the aftermath of *the best orgasm ever*, but otherwise, she seems fine.

"I have to agree, angel. It was awesome." A grin spreads my

mouth wide. "Now, let me untie you."

I help her to stand upright and begin releasing the knots, the red bindings instantly loosening around her body. A few more knots and she's unwrapped, the rope pooling at her feet. Gently, I soothe away the faint indentations across her chest with my flat palm.

"I never expected that it would feel like that," she murmurs.

Surprise, or maybe something else, makes her voice husky, and it's sexy as fuck. I wish she'd look up so I can read her expression, but her head remains lowered, following my hand. Strands of dark hair that have come undone from her ponytail form a wispy curtain over her face, further masking her from me.

Already, my cock is thickening again. The reality is that I came so hard and long I probably need a bit longer before I can think of round two. But I want a round two, three, and four. I want another whole night with this amazing woman.

"Stay with me in my apartment tonight," I whisper against the shell of her ear.

"Ryan, I can't," she says, and my hand freezes on her shoulder. "I really want to, but my sister is arriving on an early flight tomorrow morning."

Thank fuck that's the reason.

Brushing some of her hair aside, I place gentle lips against the soft skin of her neck. It's a spot that's becoming one of my favorites. "We should get you home then. It's late."

"I'll call an Uber." She shifts and stretches a little before looking around the room for her things, not bothered that we're both still completely naked.

"Let me drive you."

She opens her mouth but before she can say anything, I jump in, "Please, Charli, I want to take care of you."

Her eyebrows shoot high but I guess she sees my need to do this in my expression, because all she says in the end is, "Thank you."

SEVENTEEN

Charli

Excitement bubbles up inside me, making it impossible to stand still. My eyes are glued to the exit, searching for that first glimpse of Tori. Instead, the next person through the gates is a giant man in uniform. And the breath I'm holding is released on a loud exhale.

A woman and two little girls run toward the military man, and they're soon swallowed up in his enormous arms. It's hard not to smile at the way he captures the woman's lips with his, ignoring the tears that, even from here, I can see streaming down her face.

To find a love that special was what I dreamed of as a little girl, but I'm all grown up now, and like unicorns, I no longer believe it exists.

With a shake of my head, I try to dislodge the image of Ryan that just popped into it. The boldness of his actions last night shocked me, along with the intensity of my climax. His touch ignites a wild recklessness in me that squashes my innate cautious behavior. Nothing else matters when he's whispering into the shell of my ear, trailing his fingers through my hair, or stroking his hand down my body. All thoughts of not getting involved with my boss have been completely wiped from my mind.

I stood on the edge of the cliff that first night in his apartment, and last night, I stepped off. Now I'm free-falling, unsure if my landing will be soft or if I'll be left a crumpled, broken mess when I hit the ground.

I'm experienced enough to know a few spectacular orgasms don't mean I've found the love of my life. Besides, Ryan doesn't seem like a relationship kind of guy. I've no idea where he sees this going. Hell, I'm not even sure I know where I want it to go. All I know is that he lights me up like no one ever has before, and it's totally addictive.

My gaze skips over the crowd of other people waiting to meet family or friends arriving from various countries around the world. JFK deserves the title of New York's busiest airport.

A squeal has my head spinning in the direction of the sound. It's her, and I take off running toward my sister. We come together like two halves of a whole. Tears stream down our faces in a wave of ugly crying, but neither of us cares. Nothing matters except that we're together. Eventually, we release our tight squeeze of each other, still not speaking, just laugh-crying, as we called it growing up.

"I missed you," Tori says, hiccupping through a new wave of tears.

Grinning, I hug her tight again. "I missed you more."

Tori's watery smile beams back at me at my typical response.

This familiarity of sameness and that special feeling of being one of two are finally filling the empty space I've felt beside me ever since she left.

We eventually loosen our grip on each other enough for me to hook one arm through hers.

Tori bursts out laughing. "Look at you." She waves her hand between us, and I look down. A grin stretches my cheeks painfully wide. Of course we've dressed the same. From my new pale-blue T-shirt to the black jeans and black flats, our clothes are almost identical. This isn't unusual, as back in Sydney, we would often dress separately in our rooms, then walk out to find the other in similar clothes.

Jane didn't bother dressing us up to match as children. She said it made it harder to tell us apart. Something we always thought at least our mother would be able to do. But like everything about her, I don't think she could be bothered trying, especially when she was a few chardonnays into the evening, which was most nights. At school, the teachers made us wear different ribbons in our hair because, with our uniforms on, they were always getting us mixed up. We didn't mind. Being a matched pair made us unique in a different, special way.

The stares of other travelers barely register with either of us when we start to walk through the vast terminal. After all, for twenty-six years, we've drawn this kind of attention.

"Oh my God, I want to hear all about Ryan and the club. Everything." The words tumble from Tori's mouth at a rapid rate.

"And you have to tell me all about the cities you visited and the people you met. The photos you sent were amazing." I can't turn my thoughts into sentences fast enough.

We continue in this same way as we weave our way through the crowd, dragging Tori's bag behind us.

***

It's late afternoon by the time we're back with Sadie, gathered in the living room. Tori is propped up on one cushion of the two-seater sofa, me on the other, her legs stretched out in front of her and across my lap. We haven't been able to let each other go, and our matching features have been plastered with a grin ever since she walked through the arrival gate.

"Top up?" Sadie asks, reaching forward with the bottle of white wine. When she arrived home from work a little while ago, she insisted we all sit down and have a welcome-Tori drink together.

"I can't. I have a late shift. Any more than one glass, and I'll fall asleep on my feet later."

Sadie splashes some wine into the glass Tori holds out, then sinks back into the faded orange recliner again. It's the ugliest piece of mismatched furniture in our small living room, but it's by far the comfiest and Sadie's favorite. "Tell me about Paris. Was it better than Florence?" she asks.

Tori has just finished telling us about her travels through the ancient cities of Italy, and she doesn't hesitate to debate the point in her head before stating, "Both were amazing but for very different reasons. Paris for the food, and Florence for the men."

"How good are the French patisseries of Paris?" Sadie asks on a long, drawn-out moan. Her dream is to travel to France to eat the authentic versions of the pastries she bakes each day for the shop.

Tori laughs while patting her flat belly. "Trust me, I consumed my fair share of those. The food was amazing everywhere."

"I think I'd like Italy. Pizza and gelati, how can you go wrong?" I add. My love of pizza is well-known, and it draws a laugh from the girls.

"Aren't you tempted by the rich dark-chocolate truffles of Switzerland? They are well worth a visit," Tori adds.

Sadie jumps up with a shout of, "Popcorn."

Tori's hand jiggles, and some of the liquid in her glass spills onto her T-shirt. Her deer-in-the-headlights look makes me smile. Sadie's sudden, effusive movements can take a bit of getting used to.

"All this talk of delicious European food is making me hungry," Sadie adds as she skips toward the kitchen on a mission.

Tilting my head against the back of the sofa, I look at my sister. A warm glow fills my heart. My world seems to have righted itself and is spinning smoothly on its axis again.

"I don't know how you did it. Traveling through all those countries by yourself. I'm in awe of your adventurous spirit."

"Well, I have to live my best life because you never know—"

"Don't say it," I demand. I know the words she's going to utter, and I don't want to hear them.

Last year, Tori's boyfriend, Billy, died in a boating accident, and it changed her overnight. She couldn't wrap her head around how a fit, healthy guy with his whole life ahead of him could be gone so suddenly.

We'd already started making plans to come to New York together, but within days of his funeral, she decided to go on a grand European adventure alone instead. It was like every dream she'd ever had, every place she wanted to visit, all had to be experienced as soon as possible before it was too late.

I'm looking at her now, lounging back on the sofa like she hasn't a care in the world, and she seems transformed again. She was right to do it, even though I didn't want her to go without me. The fevered panic that filled her dark eyes when we said goodbye at Sydney International Airport has calmed to a soft, mellow brown. I could see it happening slowly every time we spoke. It was clear in her voice that each new city ticked off her bucket list was bringing her back to me.

She sighs contentedly. "Mother Nature really should have divvied up the letting-loose genes a little more fairly. You could do with having some of mine, just as some of your sensible ones would benefit me," she says.

I laugh at her summary of the situation. She's right. In this one way, we're complete opposites.

Sadie returns, carrying three bowls of hot, buttery popcorn. "Now that we have the popcorn, we can hear more about those Italian men. Or was it just that one special tall dark Italian stranger you met in Florence?" Sadie asks, waggling her eyebrows.

About a month ago, Tori excitedly FaceTimed us with stories about her sexy Italian hookup. At the mention of the man, Tori's features take on a faraway dreamy look.

"This is going to be better than a five-BON Passionflix movie," Sadie pronounces, settling farther into the cushions. "Come on. I want to hear how hot and romantic it was."

Tori smiles, but her eyes don't sparkle, and I feel her sadness. "He was my first after Billy, and that hit me harder than I thought it would." This is the first time I've heard her admit this. She'd only been dating Billy a few months, and if you'd asked either of them back then, they wouldn't have said they'd met the love of their life.

With her gaze dropped to the glass she's clutching in her hand, she continues, "He helped me through that. It was three magical days with a generous, talented lover, and I'll never forget them." She sighs heavily. "Then he had to leave."

"Will you see him again?" Sadie asks tentatively.

"Probably not. What's the point? He lives in Italy, and I live here now. That kind of distance would never work." She gives us another of her half smiles.

"But you exchanged numbers, didn't you?" I ask, realizing for the first time that this was not just a fun vacation fling like she'd tried to brush it off as at the time. While we spoke nearly every day we were apart, it was hard to pick up on her emotions, especially when it seemed like she was deliberately hiding them from me.

"Yes, but it's been a month now, and I've not heard from him. I'm thinking of deleting his number."

Right then, my cell on the coffee table buzzes with an incoming text. I check the screen, and it's impossible not to smile at the message.

"Is that Ryan?" Tori asks, seemingly happy to be able to shift the focus from her to me.

"Yes. He's asking if I still want to train tonight before my shift."

"You call it training, but I'm thinking it's just another excuse for you two to get your hands on each other," Sadie states, and I don't even try to pretend innocence.

Ryan's body pressed on top of me did feel that way before our night in his bed. But now that I know how much better it feels trapped beneath him naked, training with him is even hotter.

"Especially after last night," Tori snickers.

"What happened last night?" Sadie demands in a high-pitched tone. I haven't had a chance to update her on my orgasmic moments with Ryan behind the bar amid a sea of orgies or what happened later in his office.

"Ryan came to see me in the Red Room," I explain. Tori knows about that part of the evening, not what happened after. I wouldn't know where to begin to explain the deeply emotional experience. For now, I'm going to hold the memory in my heart until it doesn't feel so flimsy and breakable.

"And he gave her an orgasm behind the bar," Tori interrupts excitedly, and when I glare at her, she just laughs.

"What? You were in an orgy?" Sadie gasps, clutching at her chest.

"No, I was working. Until Ryan came up behind me and started talking dirty in his sexy, damn-addictive voice." I finish the dribble of wine in the bottom of my glass to wet my suddenly dry mouth before continuing, "Then one thing led to another, and he put his hand down my pants, and boom." I do a mini explosive gesture with my hand.

"Damn, I want to try that. Not with Ryan, of course," Sadie rushes to clarify. "And maybe not in an orgy room, with lots of people touching me. But the thought of having sex with a guy in public turns me on." She looks from Tori to me and back again, then shakes her head, a tumble of red curls floating about her shoulders. "What? Stop judging me."

I hold up my hand. "No judgment here. Being in the Red Room gave me an understanding of why people like it. They seemed so free to seek pleasure. Maybe you could visit the club sometime."

Sadie bounces on the chair like a toddler promised their favorite treat. "Yes, let's do that one night."

"Whoa, not me. I have to work there, but I'll ask Ryan if you can be put on the friends-of-members list."

A quick glance at Tori tells me she might not be as keen to visit the club as Sadie obviously is.

I check the time on my phone and jump up. "Sorry, girls, but I'm going to have to leave you to plan your sex club visit. I need to get ready for work."

"You mean lover boy?" Tori teases.

"Maybe. But just so we're clear there's nothing boyish about Ryan. He's all man."

"Now you're just bragging," Tori jokes. And I leave them to their chuckling as they work their way to the bottom of the wine bottle.

In my room, I reply to Ryan's text to let him know I'll be there in a half hour, then quickly start stuffing my clothes for work into my tote.

***

The minute I step into the training room a while later, the air shifts. A shirtless Ryan stands with his back to me, his head bent as he peers at his cell. His black Gi pants hanging loosely at his waist. It's a far sexier look than a guy in sweats.

I take a second step toward him, and he turns. Something in his expression tells me this isn't going to be a regular training session. Goose bumps cloak my skin, and I move toward him, eager for his touch.

EIGHTEEN

Ryan

She agreed.

Honestly, I wasn't sure she would. What Charli will say or do next always keeps me guessing. But this time, the odds were in my favor, and she agreed to meet me for our weekly training session.

Throwing a bit of my own unpredictability into the mix, I plan on this training session being a little different from the ones before. Last night, it finally felt like Charli was open to giving us a chance, and I don't want to leave it too long without consolidating those thoughts in her head.

I know she doesn't want to get involved with someone she works with, especially when I'm her boss. We agree on that point—it's not ideal. But each taste of her has me licking my lips for more. We can do this and not end up screwing up our working situation. After all, I'm nothing like that asshole, Brad.

My breath suddenly catches on a summer breeze, and I inhale deeply.

She's here.

I turn to watch her stroll toward me, our gazes locking together like magnets. I can see in her smoldering eyes that those moments in the Red Room, and later in my office, tore down more of the wall she'd erected between us. She wants this on some level, and I'm not going to deny her.

When she reaches me, I lay one hand on my gut and clutch my cell in the other. I want to touch her, but not yet. I can't remember another woman making me feel so off-kilter.

"I was just about to do a warm-up if you're ready to start?"

"You're not going to put your Gi wrap top on?" Her eyes drop to my abs.

"Not tonight. It's hot."

Her mouth pops open like she's about to say something, but instead, she bites down on her bottom lip and nods.

Turning, she drops her bag on the bench and shrugs off her sweater to reveal that tiny hot-pink crop top that appears in way too many of my dreams. I notice she doesn't take out her wrap top either, and instead, bends at the waist to remove her shoes. Surely, she's doing that deliberately, pointing her sexy-as-fuck Lycra-clad ass in my direction. My fantasies are being played out before me.

Little does she know, I plan on grappling with her on the mats in a whole different way tonight—one that would be frowned on by the martial arts masters. She's going to pay for teasing me like this.

"Ready," she declares, jutting one hip out to the side, her long fingers curled and resting on it.

We bow and step onto the thick matting, our feet leaving indents like footprints in wet sand as we pad across to the middle. Taking up our positions side-by-side, we begin with neck, shoulder, and elbow circles.

"Your sister arrived this morning?" I ask as we start to work through the standard sets of ten.

"Yes, she did, and I finally feel complete again."

I like Charli's openness with me, even if I don't always understand what she means. "Why do you say that?" I ask, shifting to squats, and in sync like a pair of choreographed dancers, we reach our hands forward and push our hips back when we dip.

"I think it's a twin thing. There's this invisible connection between us. It's like we feel what each other feels, but when Tori was so far away, the connection was weak." She stands up, shaking out her arms and legs. "I missed having her thoughts and emotions. I know that sounds weird, but that's what it feels like to me."

I reach out to brush the stray strands of hair from her face before we drop to sit on the floor to go through a series of floor twists. It's always less risky to play with her hair than to touch her skin. When it's skin on skin, I don't want to let her go.

Out of the narrow corner of my eye, I watch her twisting up onto her right knee, then rolling smoothly back and repeating the movement on the left.

"When you say you share feelings, how far does that go?"

She stops, sits on the floor, and smiles at me with a cheeky grin. "I know what you're thinking. It doesn't extend to sex. Only I get to feel that." She looks away quickly. "Just like Tori gets to keep her sexual encounters to herself."

"Good," I add, standing up and offering her a hand. Fuck, there it is, that electric charge zapping from my hand up to my chest on its way to blowing up all logical thought in my brain.

"What do you mean, then?"

"It's usually when we're sad, hurt, or scared. We can feel it."

I remember what she told me about her sister stopping her mother's boyfriend from assaulting her when she was young. Now it all makes sense.

"Well, I'm glad you feel complete again. And that your sister doesn't share your thoughts when we have sex." I drop her hand and walk over to the door, close, and lock it.

Her eyes are wide and round like chocolate drops as I walk back to join her. "Are you ready? Let's start with a full-mount Americana submission, and we'll work through it slowly."

"And the takedown?" she asks in a soft, breathy voice.

A grin pulls at the corners of my mouth. "The high crotch single leg." I've been avoiding this move and sticking to sweeping moves that can be done without having to hold her close. But tonight, I want her close. I step toward her and lift her right arm, then realize she's shaking. "Are you okay?"

"Of course," she responds, her voice firmer as she steps her legs apart to steady her balance.

Lowering my stance, I slide my right arm up her right leg to grab it. My head is tucked in close to the side of her hip, and her heart pounds in her chest beside my cheek. With both arms controlling the move, I take her down to the ground.

She lands softly on her side. My body pinning hers to mine as my legs easily maneuver her onto her back. We begin to grapple, arms and legs twisting together as we execute one move after another. Her sweat-slick body rubbing against my bare chest fills my senses with her summery-sweet scent.

I straddle her body in a full mount, my cock thickening at her nearness, and she tilts her head to the side, exposing the length of her neck. She's deliberately teasing me now. And like a Great White on *Shark Week*, I'm taking the bait.

This time, instead of completing the submission, I bend to capture her lips with mine, sucking in her soft pants and making them the air that I breathe. Our tongues tangle in a different kind of submission, neither one of us winning total control. It's like when our bodies grapple, the thrill comes from being challenged. I catch her bottom lip between my teeth, and she stills before I withdraw. Her breasts rise and fall with each rushed breath that fills her lungs. Flames burn white-hot in her gaze, daring me to do more.

With both hands, I peel the edges of her crop top up. Her gorgeous breasts now on full display, and my palms itch to close around the lush fullness. I reach out to pull on her pert dusky nipples, smiling at the sharp intake of breath when I pinch them. Bending down, I lavish the soft mounds with kisses, capturing one taut pink tip between my lips. The tang of her salty, heated skin as I circle my tongue around its peak feeds my hunger for more. She quivers beneath me and soft moans spill from her lips—those same sweet sounds from the nights in my bed and office.

I crawl down her body, working my hand under the stretch of Lycra that keeps me from my goal. I love the way the black leggings hug her like a second skin, leaving nothing to the imagination and everything to discover.

When my lips tickle a trail of kisses across her waist, she pushes up onto her elbows. "You seem to be making a habit of slipping your hand in my pants."

I peer up at her over the contours of her body. "Do you mind?"

"Not at all, as long as I get to do the same to you whenever the mood takes me."

I laugh. "Anytime, angel. Anytime."

"Good, then don't let me interrupt you."

Fuck, this woman turns me on with her mind and body. I drag the leggings off her along with her G-string, then lift a leg over each of my shoulders.

"You're leaving yourself open to a triangle choke hold," she taunts.

"Don't expect me to tap out, because I couldn't think of a better way to go than caught between your thighs with your pussy in my face." To prove my point, I hook my arms around her legs and bury my face between her thighs, licking a path through her swollen folds from her clit to her entrance.

Absolutely fucking delicious.

She's already soaking wet, and I can feel the tension in her muscles beneath my hands. Her desire coats my tongue, and I dive in to savor more of the mouthwatering taste. On the next pass, I dip into her entrance, lapping up her juices with the thirst of a man having run a marathon.

"Ryan," she whimpers, and I lift my face. "No, don't stop," she begs, her voice raspy with need. With the forty-five-degree angle that her body is at, it's impossible for her to reach my head and force the point.

I circle my tongue across the sensitive bundle of nerves, feeding two fingers into her heat. She grinds into my face until her thighs spasm around my head, and she screams out her release, the sound bouncing off the walls and fading into the cushioned flooring. I expect if there's anyone in the main part of the gym, they'll know exactly what we just did.

"Oh my God, you're good at that," Charli proclaims as she unhooks her legs from my shoulders.

I stand and try to adjust my cock in the loose Gi pants. Without compression shorts or a jockstrap to hold it down, there's no way I can hide it.

Charli waggles her brows, looking directly at my obvious erection. "Can I help you with that?"

I hold out a hand to bring her up to standing, then pass her the discarded leggings. "What are you offering?"

"Maybe a shower?"

"Great idea. You got me all hot and sweaty."

When Charli is dressed again, we grab our things and hit the showers—well, *shower*. I've never been gladder of my decision to build the set of three large showers in a way that makes them more like a hotel ensuite than what you'd find at a gym.

I lock the door behind us, and when I turn around, Charli is already undressing again. She has a gorgeous body, and I like that she doesn't feel the need to hide it. Unable to drag my eyes away, I watch her strip.

When she's done, she steps closer, and I pull her the extra foot into my arms. Her hands land on my chest, but they don't rest there for long. Soon, she's running them down to my waist and pulling the cord loose on my pants until they drop to the floor, my cock springing free. Charli glances down and laughs.

"Hey, that's not the reaction I was hoping for."

"Sorry. I was just thinking about you being commando the other times we trained together. If only I'd known there was only one piece of thin fabric between you and my mouth."

Fuck, now I'll always have that visual. I better remember my jockstrap in the future, or every training session we do will end like this one.

"There's no fabric now," I suggest, rubbing my hardened length against her flat tummy.

"And I plan on taking advantage of that," she admits, tugging me by the arm toward the shower.

A single sheet of glass separates the shower from the spacious dressing area with its sink, mirror, and wooden bench. I turn on the taps, adjusting them to the right temperature before we step in. The warm water rains on my shoulder, splashing off onto Charli's breasts before running in rivulets down her body.

From the bottle of shower gel attached to the tiles, she squeezes a glob into her hand, then rubs both hands together before bringing them to my chest. She circles them over my pecs and jokes, "Wax on, wax off."

I laugh along with her. "I'm guessing *Karate Kid* was a favorite movie?"

"Why else do you think I wanted to become a kick-ass martial arts black belt?"

She continues to trail her slippery hands over my shoulders, chest, and abs. I'm about to lose my mind with the need to be inside her, and when her hands move lower, I grab a hold of her wrists.

"I'll fucking come all over your fabulous tits if you go any further."

A fire sparks in the dark orbs she directs at me. "Well, maybe I'd like you fucking coming on my fabulous tits. Or even better, in me. Do you have a condom?"

"Don't move," I growl, then quickly grab a condom from my gym bag. Fully protected, I'm back, lifting her in my arms as the water cascades like a waterfall over our bodies. "Put your legs around my waist."

She does, and her hands grip behind my neck. The brightest, most gorgeous smile lights up her face. "I like it when you get all macho and growly at me."

"Good to know, angel." I kiss her hard, nipping at her bottom lip, then capture her gasp when her back hits the cold white tiles behind her. I position my cock at her entrance, and when her head drops to rest against the wall, exposing the long column of her neck, I whisper gruffly, "And I like it when you get all compliant," before thrusting into her.

"Fuck," she moans, and her eyelids slam shut.

"Look at me," I demand, reaching to clasp her jaw in my hand and tilting her face down. "I need you to see it's me fucking you, Charli."

Smoldering dark eyes drill into mine, and I withdraw halfway before plunging in again. This time, her lashes flutter like the wings of a butterfly but don't close.

Again, I pull my hips back, then slam in balls-deep. In, then out, stroking my cock against her tight walls. I love how her body sucks in every inch of me. She's putty in my arms, her softness molding to fit perfectly around my hardness.

My strong, confident girl handing over control to me.

That's it! Charli is my girl.

My rhythm falters to a stop at the revelation, and her gaze searches mine, demanding an explanation. And it's me who blinks first this time. It gives me a moment to reset.

"Are you ready for this?" My growl is dragged painfully up from my chest. I reach my thumb to her clit, and as soon as I touch the sensitive nub, she trembles in my arms.

Her reactions are so fucking perfect, and it sends a shot of ecstasy straight to my balls. I press her harder against the tiles, her tits squashed against my chest. The only gap between our bodies is at our hips so I can thrust my cock deep and hard into her. And I do. Over and over. My thumb rubbing circles on her nub. Her gasps turning choppier.

And when her muscles squeeze me tighter, I seal my mouth to hers, swallowing her screams at the same time as she swallows my guttural groans of release.

Fuck. She ruins me.

NINETEEN

Ryan

B*uzz! Buzz!*
Silence.
Buzz! Buzz!
Silence.

The buzzing finally penetrates my sleep instead of melding into my dreams. Angrily, I snatch up the irritating electronic device, tempted to toss it across the room. Sometimes I wish I could completely unplug from people, but my responsibilities don't allow for that.

Without bothering to open my eyes, I rub my thumb across the screen until the vibration stops. "What?" I growl and finally blink awake to see the fucker responsible for waking me up.

"Good morning, sunshine," Gio chirps close to my ear, sounding as annoyingly cheerful as one of those *Good Morning America* hosts.

I scrub my hand across my face, then see the time. "Asshole. It's five in the morning," I complain, "And I've only been asleep for two hours. What's so fucking important that you needed to call right now?"

"I'm downstairs. And while I have a key to your apartment, I figured it was safer to wake you up rather than letting myself in and you thinking I'm a home invader."

"Good choice." I sit up and throw off the covers. "Come up."

"I'm not going to see your naked ass, am I? I'm still scarred from the last time." He likes to remind me of the time he came by early one morning and strolled straight through to my bedroom, catching me buck naked, my morning wood on full display. It was embarrassing in a way that it's not when we've been in the Red Room at the same time, having sex with different women—or occasionally with the same woman.

It's been a couple of years since those days, though.

I chuckle, picking up the gray sweats and T-shirt discarded on the chair on my way to the en suite. "Not if you wait in the living room like a normal person."

The sound of the elevator door closing announces Gio's arrival while I'm washing my face. And by the time I join him, he's pulled two mugs down from a kitchen cupboard and is making us coffee. Gio is a good enough friend to know that my pre-coffee mood should be avoided.

He waits until he's handed me the mug and I've taken the first sip before saying, "Sorry for waking you up, man."

His earlier sunny demeanor has disappeared, and for the first time, I notice dark circles under his eyes, frown lines dug deep into his forehead, and his hair showing the tracks where his fingers have run through it dozens of times.

I'm not used to seeing Gio looking any way other than a contender for *GQ* Man of the Year. His dark custom-made suits, crisp white shirts, and designer ties are everyday wear for him. Certainly not the loose faded-black T-shirt and denim jeans he has on this morning.

"What's happened to you? You're dressed like you don't want to be recognized."

He runs a hand through his hair, and I guess I was right about that. "I kind of wish that was the case. That I could be incognito just for a few days."

"Does this have anything to do with your visit to your father?"

I haven't spoken to Gio since the Zoom call when he was on his way to dinner with him. It's not unusual, as we all lead busy lives and don't often get to catch up outside of our scheduled monthly business meetings.

"I think I need something stronger than coffee for this conversation."

"Dude." I look down at my watch. "It's not even six in the morning. If you want a whiskey, the Macallan is in the cupboard behind you, but count me out."

"It's not six by my body clock." He glances down at his Rolex. "I make it midday." He finds the bottle, pours himself a measure, takes a sip, and then cradles the glass instead of his coffee.

"Are you ready to tell me what's going on?"

"My father wants me to marry a family friend's daughter."

"What the fuck? That sounds like something out of the eighteen hundreds. And here I thought Italy was a modern country."

"It is. Trust me, this is not normal. It's seriously fucked up." He stares down into his whiskey like it holds the answers to the universe.

My frown deepens. I've never seen him so miserable. "Then don't do it."

He sighs heavily. "It's not that simple."

"What, you're seriously considering marrying some woman to please your father? I repeat, that's seriously fucked up."

"No, I'm not going to marry her. But I haven't figured out how to tell him that without blowing up the last vestiges of our relationship. Nobody says no to my father."

"Do you know the woman?"

"Yes, I know her. We grew up spending every summer holiday with her family in Italy. She's a friend, but there is honestly nothing else between us. If anything, I've always thought she had a thing for my brother Antonio."

"Is she attractive?" I ask, and I don't even know why. I'm so completely out of my depth with this conversation.

"I guess, but as I said, there's nothing there."

"What are you going to do?"

His head hangs low. "Honestly, man, I don't know, other than hide out here for a few days."

"What, like here in my apartment? Or Manhattan?"

"Can I stay in your spare room?" he asks, then grins when my jaw drops. "Just joking. I'll stay at Tyler Forbes's hotel."

Tyler Forbes is one of his and Hunter's friends from school, and his family owns the luxury Forbes Hotels.

"You know you could have stayed here."

"I know, but it's okay. Besides, you get angry when I drink too much of your Macallan." He pushes off from where he's been propped against the marble counter. "I'm going to go now so you can go back to bed. I'll see you soon," he says, then gulps down the last of his whiskey. Hunter would be horrified to see his favorite drink treated like it's a cheap imitation. Peering into the empty glass, Gio adds, "This is good."

"Will you come to the club tonight?" I ask as I follow him to the elevator.

"Not tonight. I'm meeting my brothers for dinner at Leo's. Hopefully, they can help me come up with a plan." Gio's three brothers are all members of the club, and I see them occasionally.

"I hope so too."

He nods. "I'll drop by the club tomorrow night. I want to see this new playroom you've been telling us about."

"Sure, it's nearly finished."

He steps into the elevator cubicle, and when the doors close, I'm left with the defeated image of my friend stamped across my brain.

TWENTY

Charli

"Cheers, ladies." Tori, Sadie, and I tap our cocktail glasses together. It's my first night off since the day Tori arrived, and we're all dressed up to party.

The pretty pink liquid is as sickly sweet as the color implies. I roll it around on my tongue, breaking down the flavors: cranberry juice, Cointreau, lime, and vodka—a traditional Cosmopolitan that's just been given a fancier name. I take another sip. No, it's not Cointreau. They've used a cheap triple sec instead, and there is way too much lime overpowering the other more subtle flavors.

Sadie and Tori stare at me, their glasses only halfway to their lips.

"What?" I demand.

Sadie laughs. "Is it that bad?" she asks, lifting the glass higher but still not bringing it to her lips.

"It's not good, but it's drinkable." I prove my point by taking another sip, and this time, they join me.

Sadie shrugs, and Tori's lips pucker.

"Tequila shots for the rest of the night?" Tori suggests.

"You can't go wrong with tequila," Sadie agrees, and we tilt our glasses together one more time before taking another teeth-clenching sip.

We dodge a drunk guy stumbling his way to the bar and move toward the seething masses on the dance floor; after all, that's what we came here for.

This trendy Midtown nightclub promised an immersive experience, and so far, it's living up to the hype. Music pounds through my body and strobing colored lights shoot overhead like bolts of lightning. All directed from the raised stage where the featured DJ and his crew tower over the gyrating crowd.

It's frenetic and exactly what I needed tonight. Maybe a little of Tori's love of adventure is rubbing off on me. We edge our way toward the dance floor with linked hands, like a mini train weaving our way through eclectic groups of people, and when we find a pocket of space, we turn to make a circle of three again.

"This place is amazing," Tori shouts, her legs beneath the black miniskirt already moving to the beat. The gold satin halter top she's wearing catches beams of light, making her sparkle. She's borrowed my spiky-heeled ankle boots, and they add an edge to the otherwise glamorous outfit.

Beside her, Sadie is in a hot-pink knit minidress, with a plunging V almost to her belly button. She has one arm raised above her head, swaying like the branches of a sapling on a windy day. She's a vibrant splash of color, an exotic flower in a sea of neutral, and in stark contrast to my black silk halter dress. Tori loaned me her gold high heels, and they make me the taller of the two of us tonight. It's nice to have an expanded closet of clothes to choose from again.

I'm jostled into Sadie by an overexuberant woman dancing beside us.

"Come on, let's dance," I shout to be heard.

We tip back our glasses, draining the contents, then place the empties on a passing waiter's tray and step farther into the throng of moving bodies. The dance floor is larger than at The Vice Club and a lot more crowded.

For the next few hours, we dance, immersing ourselves in the hypnotic beat. Stopping only a couple of times to throw back a fiery shot of tequila or chug down a glass of water before diving back into the anonymity of the crowd. We don't attempt to speak, but when we catch each other's eye, our smiles are uniformly wide. I don't remember the last time I enjoyed a night like this so much. The freedom to move my body as the music takes me and clears my mind of all other thoughts.

Tori and I have just finished drinking another water, and Sadie is chatting animatedly to the cute blond bartender. It's getting late, and a wave of tiredness washes over me when a guy steps between Tori and me.

"Well, this is certainly a double delight," he shouts to be heard over the music. The ridiculous pickup line makes my skin crawl, and I know Tori feels the same based on her dramatic eye roll. I've lost count of the number of guys who've propositioned us for a threesome over the years. Why would they think that just because we're identical twins, we'd want to share a man. Eww, it's disgusting.

Tori says something to him that I can't hear, and he disappears just as quickly as he arrived.

"Nice one," I mouth the words to her, saving my already croaky voice.

Tonight is a girls' night, and that means no guys. Not that I'm looking for a hookup. I've got Ryan.

I look at Sadie leaning farther over to whisper something in the bartender's ear. Okay, maybe she'd be up for a hookup, but I'm pretty sure Tori feels the same as me. She's been acting a little strange today, and I haven't missed the way she's been checking her cell every chance she gets. Excited nerves roll off her in waves, and I feel every one of them, but the loud music doesn't really let me ask her what's going on.

A glance at the time on my cell confirms the late hour. I'm ready to head home.

"Do you want to go?" Tori asks, leaning into me. I look toward Sadie.

"It's okay. I'll stay with her if you want to go," she adds, and I give her arm a squeeze.

Tonight's been fun, but I'm beat, and the thought of falling into my bed for an almost full night's sleep is too tempting.

TWENTY-ONE

Ryan

F*uck.*

I think I've fallen for Charli. I can't stop thinking about her. My obsession with watching her on the cameras is out of control. And with it being her night off, I'm grumpy as fuck.

It's been nearly a week since the night at the gym. With her sister now in town, and Gio arriving yesterday, we've only had a chance to see each other in the club when she's working. A few brief conversations, and even fewer opportunities to press her body to mine and kiss the living daylights out of her.

I want to take her on a date. A fancy dinner at Leonardo's like Hunter suggested. And I want to show her the newly renovated Den of Adventure. Actually, I want to do more than just show her. But none of that is possible when we don't seem to be able to find the time in our schedules.

Gio bursts into my office, not bothering to knock.

"You fucking good there?" I demand.

"Always fucking good, dude. And I know how much that grinds your gears." He certainly seems a lot cheerier than he was yesterday when he rocked up on my doorstep.

"Do I take your annoyingly good mood to mean that you sorted some shit out with your father?"

His face drops instantly into a scowl. "Not fucking likely, but today, I don't care."

Gio's ability to remain positive through adversity is a trait I admire in him. I wish I could be a little more like that instead of a broody shit when things aren't going my way.

Just like I was doing before he turned up uninvited in my office.

"Okay, so if it's not your father who put that stupid grin on your face, what did?"

"It's what's going to happen later," he replies, not elaborating any further, which can only mean one thing.

"A woman?"

He nods. "When your life has turned to shit, it's time to lose yourself in the body of a special woman."

"Since when did you become so philosophical?"

"Yesterday. When I decided sex with the right woman would give me the clarity I needed."

I shake my head but can't help smiling. The answer to my moodiness would certainly be found with Charli in my bed again. Maybe he's onto something.

"Now, how about you show me the new Den of Adventure playroom?" he asks.

"Don't go getting any ideas of using it tonight. I've got plans of my own to trial the equipment."

"Hunter said you had a woman. So who is she?"

"My new mixologist." Admitting to Gio that Charli is my woman makes me smile.

He chokes out a laugh. "Seriously? You're banging the staff, something you said you'd never do?"

"I'm not banging her, asshole. She's special," I grumble before adding, "Which is why I plan on taking her to the Den of Adventure."

"Fine. I'll stay out of the room until you've got your rope kink on with your special woman. But only if I get the next booking. I've been looking into body sex swings, and the possibilities seem endless."

I laugh. "Come on, then, let me show you what else we've installed in the room. I think you're going to like it."

***

It's well after midnight by the time I'm back in my office. Wandering through the club with the pretense of checking for any issues was pointless when I could have just checked the cameras. I'm restless without the opportunity to track down Charli. And I refuse to text her on her night off like some kind of lovesick stalker. She deserves a break from the club and me for one night.

I settle back down to deal with some of the paperwork that comes from running the club, immersing myself in the doldrums of paying invoices and renewing memberships. It's probably about time I got an assistant to help with the day-to-day administration. I've managed it until now, but with the club's increased popularity, I'm falling further and further behind. And the additional time I'm having to spend behind my desk after closing is taking its toll on me.

The last email in my inbox has been dealt with, and I switch screens to show the club cameras. Upstairs is moderately busy, with a couple of B-grade actors and their entourage. The dance floor is still packed with people dancing, and the booths are all occupied. I flick to the camera that will show me the main bar, pausing when I spot a familiar face.

Is that Charli sitting on a stool and talking to Tony? I expand the view and confirm it is. She casually recrosses one long leg over the other, and with the short black skirt she's wearing, her creamy thigh is revealed all the way up to her butt, her booted foot swinging with the beat of the music.

I check my cell to see if I missed a message to say she was coming in. No, nothing. The little minx must be planning on surprising me. I watch her pick up the cocktail glass Tony just placed in front of her on the wooden counter. It looks like her signature cocktail. I go to shut down my computer to join her when Gio enters the camera shot.

Charli turns, and a smile stretches her mouth wide. She places her glass back down, and when he reaches her side, they embrace. This is no "it's nice to meet you" hug like they've just been introduced. No, Gio's arm reaches around her, his filthy fucking hand cupping her ass while she stretches up to lace her fingers around his neck. It reminds me of how she scratched her nails into the back of my head when I fucked her in the shower.

A red haze clouds my vision. Jealousy grips my heart tight, and it feels like it's being physically ripped from my chest cavity. My fists clench tightly, nearly shattering the computer mouse in my grip. I fucking want to kill my friend for daring to touch her.

And then it hits me like a punch in the gut. She just let him.

I push off from my desk, stepping away from the computer screen that continues to play the fucking horror show, my woman and one of my best friends hooking up. I can't believe she would do this, but my eyes don't lie. It was right there on the screen. And I can't unsee it.

Anger drives my feet forward to snatch up my gym bag, and I storm out of my office. I need to fucking smash something, so I take the stairs two at a time down to the gym. It's closed now, which is what I need, privacy to unleash the fury pulsing through my body. If Charli wants to fuck someone else, then we're done. I don't share.

In the training room, I flick on every light, attempting to chase away memories of her lying on the mats screaming out her release. My black dress shirt feels like a straitjacket holding me together, and I rip it from my body, buttons pinging off and bouncing across the rubberized floor. My black pants, shoes, and socks soon follow, landing wherever they're thrown. I pull on my sweatpants, and without bothering to glove up, I step up to the heavy leather bag hanging from the ceiling by a thick chain and start punching. I rage against the wildly swinging bag, every ounce of anger leaching from my body into the pounding blows and high kicks.

The anger burns through my body with the effect of a flashbang going off, something I haven't felt since I was in my early twenties. All the skills I later learned as a US Navy SEAL to control it are forgotten in this moment.

Each blow begins to shoot arrows of pain from my curled bare fists up my arms. Yet I still don't stop. I relish the physical hurt because it means the ache in my chest is less noticeable.

But at some point, there's nothing left, and I drop to my knee on the mat beside the bag. Drenched in sweat, my heart racing, I barely have enough energy left to crawl to the nearby wall to lean against it. With my knees drawn up, my arms crossed over them and my head buried within them, I'm engulfed in the pain throbbing through my exhausted body, and I welcome it.

How long I stay like this? I've no idea. But that's how Tony finds me. A fucking miserable shell of a man.

Cheated on by the woman he was falling for.

Deceived by his friend. No, make that *friends*. Gio might not have known Charli was the woman I'd talked about earlier, but Tony, my best fucking friend, knew what she meant to me, and he just watched it happen.

"Go the fuck away," I threaten before he even has a chance to speak.

"What the fuck happened to you?" Tony growls back. If he comes any closer, I might be able to gather up the last remnants of energy to hit him. But the man has more sense and keeps his distance, recognizing the thin thread of sanity I'm still hanging on to like it's a lifeline.

"I don't fucking want to see you right now."

"Well friend, I don't care. I'm not going anywhere until you explain what kind of hell you just fell into." He sits a little farther along the wall, but still out of reach.

I don't reply.

"Ryan, what happened? Charli called me saying she couldn't reach you."

My head jolts up, and I glare at him. "I don't want to talk about her."

"Stop being a fucking idiot. She was worried about you."

"Well, that's Gio's problem now, not mine." I'm shouting now.

He stares at me like I've lost my mind, and I think I probably have. I can't believe I let a woman have this much control over me.

"You're an even bigger fucking idiot than I thought." He shakes his head, and I go to drag myself up to standing. I just found a new punching bag.

"Wait. You saw Gio with a woman you thought was Charli, right?"

"I know it was Charli. And he was pawing her like—"

"No, Ryan. It was Tori, her twin sister. Charli spoke to me about ten minutes ago and said she was at home."

He starts to laugh, and I slump back against the wall, my head dropping back with a thump as I squeeze my eyes shut. If every muscle in my body and every bone in my hands didn't hurt like a bitch, I might feel some relief at his words.

Why didn't I think of that possibility? I know she's got an identical twin sister, but stupidly, I didn't think they'd be so alike, right down to the same gestures.

"I'm going now. But not before I say my piece." He stands, looking down at my pathetic figure. "I think you owe Charli an apology for even thinking she would do something like that to you. She cares about you, asshole. Though I'm beginning to wonder why. Don't fuck this up, because it's obvious from your behavior tonight you feel the same way about her." He moves closer and leans down to squeeze my shoulder before adding, "Be the man she deserves."

Then he leaves, but his words echo in my head.

Be the man she deserves.

How do I do that? I'm not even sure I can be.

TWENTY-TWO

Charli

My first thought upon waking is to wonder if Ryan has replied to my text. When I got home from the nightclub, I messaged him to see if he wanted to train today. And I made it very clear that my suggestion of another training session meant one of his extra-special, private, all-body workouts.

Brushing my hair back from my face, I pull up to lean against the headboard and pick up my cell from the bedside table.

Tori's words from the other day about living my best life really got me thinking last night. It was somewhere between the fourth and fifth shot of tequila that it hit me. I haven't been doing that. At least not since I moved to New York.

I've just been rolling along like the little silver ball in a retro pinball machine, letting life bounce me from one thing to the next. I hated my job at Lost Paradise, but I still stayed until it became impossible to remain there. And then there was Brad. He was never a guy I was interested in, but because he asked me out on a date, I agreed, and look how that turned out.

It wasn't until I landed the job at The Vice Club that I started to feel like I was finally winning, and meeting Ryan was the cherry on top. But even now, I feel like I'm coasting, though the road is admittedly a much happier one.

It's time for me to take control in this game of life. I need to stop worrying about the what-if. Or losing sleep over what will happen next, rather than enjoying those unexpected moments of joy.

Ryan brings me joy, but constantly expecting that he will snatch it away and move on has had me holding back ... until now. The other day, I didn't hold back. It was amazing. And now I want to do that again. I've had a taste of what could be, and it's damn addictive.

His fleeting touches when he unexpectedly appears behind me as I work. The whispered promises in my ear tempting me to beg for more of his kisses. Every one of these moments builds on a sexual connection that leaves me feeling stripped naked in his arms. This special something between us can't be denied. And if I'm going to live my best life like Tori suggested, then I need to do something proactive rather than sitting back and waiting for him to make all the moves.

It's funny how letting loose on the dance floor and possibly a little too much tequila gave me that clarity. It's also why I texted Ryan.

But then he didn't respond. He always responds. And while it was before one in the morning, it's not like he wouldn't have seen it. Not a great start to my era of living my best life.

At some point overnight, my cell lost charge, as I'd forgotten to plug it in, so my screen remains completely black. I jump up to retrieve my charging cord that's slipped down beside my bed and plug it in.

When it comes to life again, a message is waiting for me.

Ryan: Can I come talk to you today?

It was sent at five this morning. What the hell was he still doing awake at that hour?

Stop, I remind myself, already doing it again—second-guessing every word of his text.

Me: I'm at home if you want to come over.

I read through the other missed message while I wait for a response. It's from Tori, saying she met up with a friend from Europe and won't be home till later. Sadie is already at work, so I've got the apartment to myself. My phone buzzes with his response.

Ryan: I'll be there in twenty minutes.

Shit, twenty minutes? That's not long. I grab clean clothes, and race to the shower. By the time Ryan is knocking at my door, I'm dressed in denim shorts and a T-shirt, and the apartment is tidy. Thank goodness Sadie and Tori are clean freaks like me.

With one deep, calming breath that does little to settle the butterflies taking flight in my stomach, I unlock the door and pull it open. Though expected, the sight of Ryan standing on the threshold of my apartment still has the power to knock the wind out of my lungs. He looks so damn good in his fitted white T-shirt stretching over every firm ridge of his abs and hugging his broad shoulders and pumped-up biceps.

My grasp on the doorknob tightens. I've no idea how we should greet each other. Do we kiss? Or hug? Or simply say hi? Nothing in his demeanor encourages me to reach up and kiss him, not even on his cheek.

"Can I come in?" he asks, holding his body unnaturally straight and still.

I nod before stepping back and nudging the door wider to let him pass. I concentrate on the play of muscles bunched under the thin white fabric as I follow him the short distance to the living room. It seems impossible that it was less than a week ago that I was able to run my soapy palms freely over those same muscles. Nothing in his posture would dare me to reach out to him today.

He fills the space—not physically but with his presence—which sucks the air from my lungs.

"Do you want to sit?" I ask, and once he's folded his body onto the sofa, I push on through the awkward silence. "You wanted to talk to me."

"Please sit beside me?" he asks in a low, deep voice, and I do.

He's on one cushion, and I'm on the other as I tilt my body toward him, tucking one leg underneath me.

He leans forward with his elbows on his knees, then turns his head to face me. "I owe you an apology."

My brows rise. I don't know why he's come to see me, but I didn't expect him to start with that. "Why?"

His fingers link together, and for the first time since he walked through my door, I notice the bandages wrapped over his knuckles. "Last night when I was going through the cameras, I saw a woman at the main bar that I thought was you."

"Tori?" I ask, leaning closer.

Why was Tori at the club? And why didn't she tell me?

He continues, "I guess. Anyway, she and Gio kissed." His jaw tightens. "I thought it was you … and I lost my shit." He drops his head, rubbing his hands across his face.

There are so many questions swirling around in my head, but I settle on voicing the simplest. "Who's Gio?"

"My friend," he replies just as simply.

I've no idea how Tori knows Ryan's friend Gio. She's never mentioned that name, and I don't like the thought that there are things she's not told me. "Go on," I encourage.

He releases a heavy sigh. "I thought you and Gio were hooking up."

"What?" I snap, my head jerking up to stare at him. He thought I was cheating on him? "Why would you think that?" I demand. "I would never fool around with one guy when I'm having sex with another. I thought you understood that about me." It hurts to know he thought I would do that.

"And that's why I owe you an apology," he explains. "I'm sorry. I should have known that wasn't the type of person you are." He reaches for my hand, and I don't pull it away, but I also don't let him link his fingers through mine. Instead, I take a few deep breaths, then look down at where his larger hand rests over mine.

My gaze narrows. "What happened to your hands?"

"I beat the hell out of one of the heavy punching bags instead of my friend." He shifts his gaze up to capture mine. "I was so fucking angry."

"Why?" I whisper, and the shades of blue in his irises darken.

"Because the thought of another man touching you drove me insane." His voice is firmer now. The words cutting through me like a knife through butter and leaving me open to possibilities. A breath catches in my chest as I imagine another what-if. Not the kind that leads to *what if something bad happens*. But the kind that sets the butterflies in my stomach flapping even more frantically than before.

My gaze drops to where his hand remains on mine, light as a feather but with a heat that scorches a path to my soul. Ryan has always been different. Special. From the first day when he held me steady by my hips. Even then, I trusted him to not let me fall. Now I need to make him see that he can trust me back.

Ryan feels like my best life, and it's time I started living it rather than tiptoeing around the edges. This man pummeled a bag to the point of injury because he thought I wasn't interested in him anymore. It's a sweet kind of messed up.

Slowly, I turn my hand over to curl my fingers around the edges of his palm, then with my other, I gently brush my thumb over his knuckles. "Do they hurt?"

The corners of his mouth twitch. "Fuck yes."

"That was a stupid thing to do without gloves."

"I know." He tilts his head from side to side. "You're not the first person to tell me that."

"Tony?" I smile at him.

"Of course. That guy likes nothing better than telling me I'm a fucking idiot." His hand grips mine tighter, and his gaze is like two laser pointers. "You know what else he told me?" he asks in a low voice that no longer has a hint of humor.

I hold my breath, waiting for him to continue.

"He told me to be the man you deserve."

My mouth drops open on an exhale.

"That's what I want more than anything, but I've got no idea how to be in a relationship … obviously." He holds his other hand up with his knuckles facing me.

The pounding of my heart fills my chest to bursting. My best life feels like it just got even better. I've seriously fallen for this man.

"Tony is a wise, good friend." I edge my butt closer to him before placing one hand on his shoulder, pushing him back against the cushions, then lifting up to straddle his hips. His hands immediately land on my hips, exactly where they've always belonged.

Threading my fingers around the back of his neck, I pull his head to me, sealing my lips to his. Our tongues search and find each other as the kiss becomes hard and demanding. In equal parts, I give and take.

His warm palms inch under the hem of my T-shirt, feather-soft touches that make me wriggle beneath them. Delicious shivers radiate from each point of contact, rippling just below the surface of my skin. Ryan affects me like no other man ever has. His skillful hands slide higher to cup my braless breasts, and waves of heat flow from his massaging fingers to my tits as I push my chest into them.

When he pinches the taut tips, he swallows my moans. My thighs clench around his hips, and I rock against his hard shaft.

Click! Click! Squeak!

The sound of the apartment door opening has us springing apart. Ryan's hands return to my hips, and my rolled-up T-shirt falls to land over them.

"Hey, I'm home," Tori calls out from the hall, and then, over Ryan's shoulder, I watch her come to a screeching stop in the doorway.

"Oops. Sorry for interrupting." The huge grin plastered across her face makes the word *sorry* seem like a lie. She's loving catching me all hot and heavy with Ryan. Her keys clatter on the kitchen counter, and my eyes close with the hope she'll go to her room. But the sound of her boots on the floorboards tells me she's coming closer, not leaving, and my eyes spring open as she walks into Ryan's line of sight.

"Fuck," Ryan mutters, looking between Tori and me, his jaw dropped. "You really do look identical."

I slap him lightly on his chest and roll my eyes.

Tori steps closer. "I'm assuming this is Ryan, your boss?" she asks, waggling her eyebrows.

Beneath me, Ryan's cock presses firmly against my denim shorts, ensuring I stay planted in his lap.

Instead, I glare at her over my shoulder. "Of course this is Ryan. And don't you try to be shocked by my behavior when I've just found out that *the friend* you stayed with last night was a guy named Gio."

Her mouth drops open, and a blush tinges her cheeks pink.

My grin is smug. "I've got so many questions for you."

She recovers quickly, as I knew she would. It's a rare occurrence for Tori to show signs of embarrassment, which makes her initial reaction even more intriguing.

Mischief twinkles in her eyes as she smirks. "Probably, but it seems to me like you might have your hands full." She waves a hand between us. "So I guess those questions will have to wait." She spins on her toes and walks away, shouting back, "It was nice to meet you, Ryan. I'm sure I'll be seeing a lot more of you in the future … now that you and my sister seem to be official."

What the hell? I'm going to kill her. I drop my head to Ryan's chest, hiding a blush of my own.

A chuckle rumbles up from his belly, earning him another playful slap.

When he's finally got a grip on his amusement, he asks, "Is she right? Because I sure want us to be official."

I peer up at him through a curtain of messy hair. "What does that even mean? It's not like we're a couple of teenagers."

"It means that I would like to take you out to dinner. On a proper date." His hands slip back under my T-shirt, stroking up my bare skin until they are again cupping my breasts, his thumbs rubbing over my taut nipples.

"I think I'd like that," I admit, melting under his touch. "Does it also mean we can have some more private training sessions?"

He nods, placing a string of kisses from my collarbone up to my neck. I tilt my head to the side, giving him better access.

"And that you'll give me the extended tour of the Den of Adventure?"

"Fuck yes. It definitely means that and a whole lot more." His mouth trails more light pecks along my jaw, eventually reaching mine. I pull him into a hard, mind-blowing kiss, and it's a long while before we speak again.

Sadly, with my sister only in the other room of our tiny

apartment, our sexy activities are limited, and when he's extracted a promise from me to visit him in his office tonight, he leaves.

The door shuts with a bang behind him, and I waste no time hunting Tori down to find out what's going on between her and Ryan's friend Gio.

TWENTY-THREE

Ryan

"I want you in my office. Now," I demand.

Charli's response is quick and even briefer. "Sure, Boss. Will do."

Desire surges through me at her tone, and I hang up.

Patience is a virtue I've no time for tonight. We've got unfinished business from earlier when her sister unintentionally cock-blocked me by arriving home, ending any chance of us getting naked. But with her shift nearly finished, I'm not waiting a moment longer for her to be in my arms again. Charli belongs in my arms, in my bed, and anywhere else she'll allow me to take her.

Every chance I could get tonight, I've spent it with her. She was working in the main bar, so that's where I was for hours. It's been years since I poured drinks, and while I can't do all the fancy cocktails like Tony and Charli make, bartending is where I started. I forgot how enjoyable it could be chatting with the customers. It beats sitting up in my ivory tower, out of touch with the reality of the club. Maybe I need to do this more often.

Although it's been torture watching her and not touching, it's worse not being near. The way she bites her bottom lip as she carefully measures spirits and mixers into the silver shaker. Every movement is precise and graceful as she reaches for a bottle, bends for a glass, and steps from one foot to the other as she blends her unique concoctions. She's like a performer executing a complicated choreographed dance. The final result is poured in a tall glass or a short, squat one and is guaranteed to be a little piece of magic that will tease and tempt your taste buds.

Charli's cocktails have been a huge hit with the patrons, and having tasted her signature saffron-infused one, I can see why.

I follow her progress through the different cameras as she makes her way to my office. Her sexy black jeans are worn like a second skin, hugging her shapely butt, and the new tiny diamanté-encrusted bra top is jaw-droppingly spectacular. I want to lick a path across the creamy strip of exposed skin along her midriff. Especially when I know that it will probably extract one of her soft moans or chase goose bumps across her stomach.

She knows what she does to me, and I'm sure tonight's outfit was carefully selected for maximum impact. My naughty little angel is challenging me again. I like it.

One, two, three. And there is the knock. A short rap, yet there is nothing tentative about the woman on the other side.

"Come in," I command in a deep, low voice.

A smile teases the corners of her mouth as she enters. "You want me, Boss?"

"Always," I admit from where I'm leaning against the edge of my desk, then add in a gravelly voice, "Come here," when she stops just inside the room.

She struts toward me but, this time, stops a couple of feet away. "Maybe you need to come here." She curls her finger to beckon me closer.

Every time she speaks, whether she means to or not, her sassy words turn me on even more. And every time she's near, I have to touch her, like a magnet drawing me closer, it's impossible to resist.

I reach out one arm and hook it around her waist, pulling her the rest of the way to me, and her hands land softly against my chest. This is where she belongs, in my arms.

She looks up at me, and I wonder at the devilish glint in her dark eyes. "Are you feeling adventurous? Because I am." Those words laced with hidden meaning in her husky voice make my cock stand up and pay attention.

When I agreed to take her to the new playroom, I didn't realize she meant tonight. But now, hope grows like the tendrils of a vine twisting through my chest and squeezing around my heart. Fuck yes, I want to play.

"You're going to need to be a little clearer in what you're asking for, angel." I trace a finger across her warm skin, outlining the edge of her top and remembering a silk rope binding her chest right there. My finger continues to draw a path down between the curve of her breasts. The Shinju chest harness was striking against her smooth satin skin here. Her breath catches as I dip into her cleavage.

She reaches up to cup my jaw, her soft palm resting against my day-old stubble.

"Tonight," she begins slowly, her hand scrapping across my chin. "I want you to take me to the new playroom and have sex with me ... in the swing."

That's clear, but one thing she said doesn't sit comfortably with me. I grip her hand and, tilting my head, place a kiss on her palm. "Tonight, we won't just have sex." Another kiss. "Tonight, I am going to make love to you." Again, I full stop the sentence with my mouth against her flesh. "Slowly and passionately. You and I have never been only about sex. With you, it's always felt like so much more. *You* are so much more."

"I think I'm falling for you," she murmurs.

"I know I've fallen for you," I admit while reaching down to take her other hand. "And I'd very much like to show you what that means."

Hand in hand, we walk silently to the playroom. There's no one else around on this level, as the club has just closed. Tony agreed to finish up downstairs, and I told him I didn't want to be disturbed on this level. He knew what I meant when we spoke this afternoon.

He was another person I needed to apologize to after my meltdown last night. He accepted it but couldn't resist dealing me another dose of Tony's wise words, coated in laughter: "That's what happens when you fall in love. You do stupid shit."

It's hard to argue that point. I am in love with Charli, but I don't want to say those words to her until I can take her on a real date. Given that I've never uttered them to another woman, they are huge words for me, with big feelings behind them.

The door clicks open with a swipe of my keycard, and I usher her in ahead of me before turning on the central spotlight. Her gaze locks on the swing harness hanging from the thick gold chain in the center of the room.

She's caught me by surprise again with her request to visit the playroom, so I haven't prepared anything special for her. But given the way she's chewing on her bottom lip, that's probably a good thing. She stands like a gorgeous contradiction, one hand on her hip, the other rubbing a path up and down her jean leg.

"What happens now?" she whispers, continuing to stare at the swing. "Do I undress and you hook me up?"

After dimming the spotlight so it's a more ambient level, I move to stand in front of her, placing my hands on her shoulders. "First you relax, angel."

Her gaze fixes to mine, and already, her quick breaths are slowing to a more natural rhythm.

"Good girl."

A gentle kiss on her soft lips eases the remaining tension from her shoulders.

"Would you like a drink? Champagne? Water? Or something else?"

"Water, please," she says, walking farther into the room.

From the mini fridge near the door, I grab two small bottles out and hand her one. Her gaze flits around from one thing to the next, her brain seeming to struggle to take it all in.

The newly installed bamboo pole attached diagonally across one corner of the room—for use in Shibari suspension bondage—snags her gaze for a moment. Next is the metal ring on another gold chain hanging from the ceiling, and she looks away quickly. Finally, her eyes rest on the tan leather Tantra Chair against the side wall.

"Speak to me, Charli. I need to know what's going through that beautiful mind of yours."

She turns to me. "Honestly, I'm a little overwhelmed by all of this." Her hand swipes through the air. "I thought I'd be cool about doing this kind of thing, but now I'm a little nervous. I don't even know what some of this stuff is, so I've no clue how we would use it." She bites down on her bottom lip.

I step closer and brush my thumb across the pillowy softness, releasing it from her teeth. "We can stop at any time. Everything in this room is about pleasure, and if you feel uncomfortable, we can try something else or leave."

"Okay," she murmurs so softly I can barely hear the

acknowledgment. Her throat bobs on a gulp of water before she asks more clearly, "Can you explain that?" She nods toward the swing.

"A body sex swing is a little like a life jacket with additional straps to support the butt and legs. It allows for more interesting and challenging sexual positions."

"It's not like any life jacket I've ever used."

Chuckling, I watch as she turns away from the swing and wanders over to the chair. Her gaze on the wall behind it. It holds a series of twelve gold-framed erotic photos. Naked men and women bound with rope, some suspended in the air by intricate knots, and others more simply tied standing or kneeling.

She returns her gaze to mine, and with a nod of her head toward the photos, she murmurs, "Is this like a menu of options? Because I think I'd like this."

My grin is broad as her gaze drops to the chair. It's the least scary piece of furniture in the room.

"Have you seen a Tantra Chair before?" I ask, resisting the urge to crowd her.

"Only on the internet." She trails her fingers over the leather back. "I like the sweeping curve of it. It looks sexy but comfortable."

"It is," I agree, moving to stand behind her. I sweep her ponytail over one shoulder before peppering kisses across the other and up the long column of her neck. She leans back into my body, tilting her head to the side and giving me better access.

With my arm around her waist, I turn her to face me. "What do you want to do?"

"Well, I do like a challenge," she teases.

Laughter rumbles up through my chest and bursts out of me in a loud cough that makes her jump. "And don't I know it."

She rolls her eyes before continuing, "My favorite thing on playgrounds as a child was the swing. So I think I might like to play on your swing." Her earlier nerves have disappeared like I knew they would.

"I always liked the swing too."

"Funny, I'd have thought you would have been more into rope courses." She gives me a cheeky wink.

Another laugh rumbles to the surface. Fuck, I love this woman, and squeezing her body to mine, I seal my mouth to hers. She trembles in my arms as I ease her over the high back of the chair. Our tongues tangle, tasting and sucking, and heat immediately ignites my blood with the ferocity of a wildfire.

My fingers find the button on her jeans, slide the zipper down, and unhook the fabric slowly from her hips. She reclines over the curve of the chair, and I hook an arm under her knee to lift one leg and remove her boot. Then do the same with the other, massaging each foot as I do.

Her eyes flutter closed like she's tasting her favorite cocktail. "Hmm, what you're doing to my foot feels amazing."

"As much as I love these sexy boots, maybe you need something more comfortable to wear during your shifts."

A soft moan slips from her lips as I dig my thumbs into the arch. "I'd agree to anything when you're doing that."

"Good to know for now and in the future."

She looks so beautifully relaxed, her back arched over the chair, eyes closed, and her arms flung above her head.

With her boots discarded, I peel the jeans down. My kisses are scattered like sprinkled fairy dust over each exposed inch of skin, all the way down to her blood-red-painted toes. I remove my clothes except for my black boxer briefs, which are being stretched impossibly tight against my fully erect cock. It's best I keep these on for the moment. Then, kneeling at the end of the chair between her legs, I hook my fingers into the elastic band of the scrap of lace covering her. I'm tempted to rip it off, but I suspect she won't appreciate losing another piece of underwear to my impatience. It looks so pretty on her that I ease it off instead. She's fully exposed to me, and with both hands on her hips, I glide her closer along the soft leather until her creamy thighs are spread around my head. I blow a breath against her glistening folds, and her hips arch her closer to my lips. A groan leaps through my throat as I flatten my tongue to lap at her soaked core. Stroking from the top to her entrance and occasionally sucking on her clit.

Over and over, I tease her swollen flesh.

I don't let up the pleasure—taking her to the edge, then retreating—until she's writhing beneath me and threatening all kinds of tortuous revenge if I don't let her finish. I relent. And this time when her hips buck and demand more, I don't stop until her climax barrels through her body in a violent shiver. Her moans fill the room, the muscles in her thighs tensing beneath my palms and mouth.

Without giving her a moment to recover, I lift her from the chair and carry her to the swing, feeding her limp limbs into the harness. The touch of the leather against her skin seems to reinvigorate her, and she sits high in the swing, her long fingers gripping the straps, her gaze wide-eyed and glued to me. A smile paints her lips still swollen from my kisses. She looks gorgeous suspended, open and waiting for me.

I'm transfixed. The diamantés on her top catch the outer edges of the spotlight and dance colored beams around her.

"I like your new top," I grind out.

"I thought you might," she admits, confirming my earlier suspicion that she had worn it specifically to get a reaction from me.

A muscle in my chest tugs, and I suspect it's the result of the rate at which my heart races. I want her to think of me when she dresses. Actually, I want her to think of me every waking hour and in her dreams when she sleeps.

Charli, my woman, is everything I need. And I want to be the man she deserves.

I rip off my boxers and cover myself with a condom. The temptation to fill her, joining our bodies together, is overwhelming. So, with only one stroke through her folds to coat me, I cup her ass in my hands and swing her toward me as I thrust into her in one smooth movement.

"Fuck," she shouts, as her walls stretch around me, locking my body within her heat like she never wants to let me go. Something I'm definitely okay with. Her chest rises and falls with each labored breath.

"I'm floating on your cock," she pants, her head turned to the side to face the large floor-to-ceiling antiqued mirror, watching our bodies come together.

Our gazes find each other in the reflection. "That's right. Just like the sexy little angel you are." I swing her onto my shaft harder.

"Ohhh, do that again," she begs, and I do, again and again. She leans back into the swing, and it tilts her hips higher, changing the angle of my thrusts.

"Fuck! Yes. More."

Giving her more is easy when I want to give her everything.

Her body slaps against mine, and I reach out to rub her clit.

My balls draw up, and her inner muscles tighten their hold on me. The squeeze is so intense my vision clouds and I can't hold on. I rub harder, wanting her with me as I go over the edge.

And then I'm coming. And her walls are closing around me impossibly tight as she falls too. My sight narrows to a pinprick of light, a light that's filled entirely with Charli. The sound of her soft moans. The touch of her velvety skin. The scent of her breezy perfume mixing with our release.

The pleasure is almost too much to remain standing. But somehow, I do, because I can't let go.

I never want to let her go.

TWENTY-FOUR
Charli

"You're very quiet," Ryan murmurs from behind me.

He's just released me from the swing, and while I'm standing, it's only barely, as my legs feel shaky and weak. Not surprising when I've just had two of the most amazing, intense orgasms of my life.

"Probably because you fucked the words right out of me." A satisfied smile that will take days to wipe away makes my cheeks ache.

He chuckles. "I make you speechless. I like that."

I turn, and he's standing there naked, looking like a statue of Adonis, his muscled body pure perfection. I lean my forehead into the solid wall of his chest, and his hand burrows into my hair to cup my head. His other arm is around my waist, supporting me. It's such a sweet, gentle move after the frenetic activity of the last hour that it almost makes me cry with the fullness of emotions. And I've never been a crier, sad or happy.

Ryan has the ability to squeeze previously undiscovered emotions from me, leaving me as weak and unsteady as a newborn baby lamb.

"Are you okay?"

"Mmm, more than okay." With a slight tilt of my head, I peer at him through half-closed eyes.

"Come on, let's get you to bed," he says before placing a light kiss on my head.

He walks me to the chair, then gathers my clothes and hands them to me. But dressing requires too much energy, and instead, I snatch up Ryan's T-shirt and pop it on over my head.

"It suits you," he says, grinning as he pulls his jeans on commando. Damn, that's hot.

"Do we need to clean up in here?" I ask.

"No, the cleaners come in the morning. Did you get everything?"

"I think so," I reply, looking down at my jeans and boots in my hand.

He bends to pick up something from behind the chair and comes up grinning, holding my G-string. But he doesn't give it to me, tucking it into the back pocket of his jeans instead. Then, taking my free hand, he leads me from the playroom, turning off the light and locking the door again.

"Can we do that again sometime?"

"We can go to the playrooms anytime you want, as long as you let me take you to my bed after," he agrees, this time, sealing his words with a light kiss on my lips. It's too brief, and standing on my toes, I reach one hand to pull him back to me, pressing my mouth to his, my tongue venturing between his lips to deepen it.

He groans deeply, pulling away enough to bury his face in my neck. "Fuck, woman, if you keep that up, I'll have you bent over a bar stool rather than in my bed." He lifts his head, and his gaze is like laser beams of light drilling into me. "Now I need you to wait here while I check the doors are locked and set the alarms."

I nod, plonking myself on the closest stool at the VIP bar. And true to his word, Ryan's back about five minutes later, my tote in his hands.

"I thought you'd want this."

I smile my thanks and fall a little bit more for him. He makes me feel special, cared for, in a way that I've never felt before. When I stretch my arm around his waist, his automatically slips over mine, my body slotting together with his as naturally as taking my next breath, and as with every touch, the butterflies in my stomach flutter to life, recognizing his warmth.

"Can you take me to your bed now?" I ask. A tiny kiss dropped to my forehead is his only answer before he leads me upstairs.

This is my second time in his apartment, but it feels like the first as I look around. I'd not paid my surroundings much attention last time, given what had happened. The open-plan living area is New York-loft style, with soaring ceilings and large wooden beams running across the expanse. There is an exposed brick wall at one end of the room, while the rest are plastered and painted pure white. The starkness of the finishes is softened by the two oversized comfy cream sofas in the middle of the space, a distressed vintage rust-colored rug between them.

"A drink first?" he asks from the kitchen area, where he empties his pockets of a bunch of keys, his cell, and a wallet. "Or straight to bed?"

The temptation to answer "bed" is still there, but I also like the idea of us sitting together on the sofa talking. There's still so much I don't know about him. And I want to know everything—or at least all the important bits.

"Are you offering a Macallan again? Or was that only in special circumstances?"

He chuckles. "Having you in my apartment is always special," he tells me as he reaches into a cupboard to get a couple of glasses.

"I bet you say that to all the women," I try to joke, but even to my own ears, it lands flatter than a pancake.

There goes my mouth, running off before engaging my brain because he told me last time that he doesn't bring women to his apartment. I don't want to sound pathetically insecure, even if I'm feeling it. I've fallen hard for Ryan, and it's a little scary how vulnerable and confused it makes me feel.

In the kitchen, Ryan has placed the glasses on the counter and is striding toward me. He doesn't stop till he's wrapped his arms around me and has captured my mouth in a kiss that is rough and deliciously demanding. But as I sink into his blissful taste, he just as quickly snatches his lips away.

"Charli, we need to get a few things straight between us. Maybe you've forgotten, but I'll remind you. I have never, and I mean never, invited another woman up to my apartment and, more specifically, my bed. You are the first and only woman I want in my private space. You are the woman I'm going fucking crazy for. Only you."

When I manage to pick my jaw up, I say the first thing that pops into my head. "Then *you* need to take me to your bed. Right now."

Before I know what's happening, I'm swung into the air and hanging upside down over his shoulder.

For once, speaking without thinking is paying off for me.

TWENTY-FIVE

Ryan

"To us." A simple toast reflecting what's taken root in my heart, and I hold my breath, waiting to see Charli's reaction.

She raises her crystal champagne flute and taps it with a ting against mine, her expression softening into a smile as her brown eyes, shining like tempered dark chocolate, find mine.

"To us … dating?" Her low voice rises in question. The breath I'm holding whooshes from my body. I don't like that she sounds a little unsure.

"The first of many," I suggest, making clear my intentions.

She tilts her head from side to side, her soft, glossy waves bouncing about her bare shoulders.

"I guess I could get used to this." A cheeky wink is the full stop to her words before her gaze flicks to the tall columns of twinkling colored lights through the large floor-to-ceiling windows. Our candlelit table, covered in starched, crisp white linen, is shielded from others by a curved partition of thin oak strips and is angled toward the unrivaled city view. The layout gives us a level of privacy you rarely find in a restaurant and is one of many reasons for its popularity.

Another is the food, and it's immediately apparent why as the first plate from the tasting menu is placed in front of us. The three grilled scallops on a bed of celeriac and apple slaw is a little work of art decorated with daubs of a tangy lime-green sauce. It pairs beautifully with the chilled glass of Krug.

I know how important finding the perfect mix is to Charli, and this meal promises to meet every one of her measures in presentation, scent, and flavor. I place my fork back on the table and watch her taste the first morsel of food in her mouth. If the soft sigh is any indication, I'd say she likes it. The problem is her expression is reminding me of when she makes similar mewling sounds just before she climaxes, and I use the cover of the linen serviette on my lap to readjust my thickening cock beneath it.

In an effort to distract my wayward thoughts, I ask, "Did I tell you this restaurant is owned by Gio's brother, Leo?" I probably did mention this in the intervening days between my promising to take her on a date and tonight actually happening. But it has the desired effect of stopping me from wanting to clear everything from the table so I can lay Charli across it. She makes me feel unhinged.

"You did. Although it's Gio I'm more interested in than his brother." Her brow creases in thought. "Tori is reluctant to speak about him since he returned to Italy. It's not like her."

Gio seems reluctant to speak to me about her too. He left in a rush, giving me the impression that he needed space, so that's what I'm giving him. I'm not even sure when he's planning on coming back.

"I'd rather not talk about another guy when we're on a date."

"Good point," she agrees, then places her elbow on the table and rests her chin in her palm. "So let's talk about you, then." For some reason, I feel like I've been conned, and her intention all along was to get me to open up. Clever girl. I walked right into that trap.

Over the remaining courses, I open up to her about my mother's battle with alcoholism, being shunted between her and my grandparents', and being made to feel like an unwanted piece of old clothing. It's not a light, entertaining topic. Especially when Charli adds her own similar experiences. But it's an important conversation that's long overdue, and I share things about my life I've never told another person.

By the time we leave, only the staff remain.

"That was delicious," Charli proclaims as I lead her from the restaurant with my hand on the small of her bare back.

From behind her, I hold her coat open, and she slips her arms into the sleeves, covering her sexy new dress. The thought of removing the mid-length black satin sheath has had me semihard all night. The combination of demure and sophisticated at the front and pure seductress with the low scooping back a perfect reflection of her personality. She scoops up a handful of hair caught underneath the collar of her coat and places it over her shoulder, allowing me a chance to trail my fingers along the exposed column of soft skin on the other. Her lashes drop before opening back up to reveal dark, smoldering orbs. She's pretending to be unmoved, but I know her tells now.

Close to her ear, I whisper, "Would you like to come back to my place?"

"The club?" She turns in the circle of my arms.

"No, my apartment. In my bed."

"On a first date?"

"I figured we'd moved way beyond first-date rules. It's time I romanced you."

A cheeky grin splits her cheeks. "What is this romance you speak of?"

I stroke one finger softly along her jaw. "Slow, steamy lovemaking."

She melds her body with mine. "But what if I want it hard, rough, and dirty?"

I cough out a laugh. "Then that's exactly what you'll get for your first orgasm, and the second one will be slow."

"And the third?" she jokes.

"Fuck, do you have any idea how crazy I am for you?"

Her hand brushes across my cock. "Maybe some."

Grabbing the same hand, I tug her toward my waiting town car. "We're out of here. Before I drop you to your knees and feed you my cock. Right here on the sidewalk."

"Is that a promise?"

That sexy, dirty mouth of hers will be the death of me.

"You better believe it," I say as I open the car door for her. It's exactly what I plan on doing the second we're in my apartment. My feisty girlfriend needs a lesson in what happens when she teases her boyfriend.

When she's settled on the back seat, I follow her, sliding in close and crowding her against the other door. I slip my arm under her coat, wrapping it tightly around her waist and placing my other hand at her neck. Her skin is warm under the slippery satin of her dress, and I bet she's already soaking wet. I trail my flat palm down over the swell of her breast. Her gasp captured in the seal of my mouth to hers. Our tongues duel, and like it is when we're grappling on the mats, we share control of the kiss equally. And when I rub my thumb across her pebbled nipple, she melts back into the seat with a needy groan. She couldn't be more perfect.

"I love that," I murmur, leaning in to pepper kisses along the exposed column of her neck.

But her head springs up off the headrest, nearly headbutting me. "What did you say?" she asks in an urgent whisper.

"I said I love that ... those little noises you make when I touch you."

She slumps back against the seat, tilting her face toward the window. "Ohhh," she murmurs, drawing out the small word into a longer-sounding one.

"Charli." I place my hand on her cheek and turn her to face me. The streetlights illuminate her features, and she's never looked more vulnerable or beautiful. "You have the innocent face of an angel, the dirty mind of a devil, and an adventurous spirit that speaks to my heart. I love all your contradictions, your strength, and those times when you get quiet because you're unsure. I had planned to do this in a more romantic setting than the back seat of a car, but fuck it. I love you, Charli. I have for a while now."

She twists in my embrace, turning to face me. "I love you too, Ryan. I know that me saying it after you might seem like I don't mean it. But I do." She throws her arms awkwardly around my neck, restrained from a grand gesture by her seat belt. She unhooks her arm from the strap and succeeds this time.

"See what I mean? Not the most romantic setting." I groan, doing my best to bring our bodies closer together and failing.

"I don't care. All that matters is that you love me. Ryan, you're everything I wished I could find in a guy but had begun to think didn't exist. Trustworthy, kind, and sexy as hell."

"Are you saying I'm your perfect mix?" I joke.

"Yes, my perfect mix," she says before pulling me in for another of her mind-blowing kisses.

And when the car pulls up outside my apartment a little while later, we're ready to shake things up.

EPILOGUE

Ryan

Four Months Later

"That's hot," Tony mutters from where he's leaning against the training room wall. I backhand my friend in the gut so quickly he doesn't have a chance to block the blow.

"Oomph!" he grunts, and I get some satisfaction from the sound.

We're watching the girls grapple on the mats after having just finished a punishing workout on the punching bags. He's right; Charli looks so fucking sexy, her leg muscles straining as she twists her strong, nimble body a full ninety degrees to escape from Tori's attempt to restrain her.

Still, I feel the need to reprimand him. "Shut the fuck up, dude. That's my girlfriend you're talking about."

Tony rubs a hand across the front of his white tank top as a low chuckle rumbles up from his chest. He knows that mentioning Charli in any remotely sexual way triggers this kind of reaction, so he makes it his mission to tease me regularly. He also thinks I need to loosen up a little and give her space to breathe. I get that sometimes I'm overprotective and, to my mind, with good reason after the incident with Brad. Though, I do try to let her handle situations with customers in the club herself.

"I thought you'd got all the punching out of your system with the bag," he accuses, still grinning.

With a sideways glance in his direction, I reply, "No, I always like to keep one in reserve just for you," and he laughs harder.

"You're only in a bad mood because you didn't get a chance to roll around on the mats with Charli yourself."

Maybe he's right. The four of us often train together, switching up the combination of pairs and swapping between the mats and the bags. I had hoped that Charli and I could train together today, especially as she didn't stay over last night. It's never a good day when I wake up without her in my bed. But hopefully that won't be the case for much longer.

I rub a small towel over my face and head, swiping at the beads of sweat dripping down.

"I'm going to ask Charli to move in with me," I mutter, keeping my voice low so only he can hear me. "Do you think she'll agree?"

"Of course she will, the girl's crazy about you," he says, immediately quietening the kernel of doubt that is ever present thanks to my dysfunctional upbringing. Pushing off from the wall beside me, he turns to face me. "I'm happy for you, man."

"Thanks," I mumble, looking away. I appreciate my friend's endorsement, but I'm still uncomfortable with this kind of emotional sharing stuff. Although I'm getting better at it with Charli's help.

"I'll catch you later," he says with a hard slap on my shoulder. "And tell Charli, not to rush, I'll do the open in the main bar," he adds before wandering over to the bench to collect his gear and heading in the direction of the showers.

I'm glad that Tony and Charli, the two people closest to me, have become good friends; even though I was initially a little jealous of the time they spent together. I realize she needs to be her own person without me constantly hovering, so most nights, I don't even see her until she knocks on my office door at the end of her shift. I've even stopped stalking her through the cameras and making surprise visits while she's working—except for those nights when she's in the Red Room, and she asks me to drop by. I live for those stolen moments, watching her come undone as I pleasure her hidden from view by the solid marble counter.

In the beginning, there were so many reasons why I should have stayed away from Charli. I was her boss, there was a ten-year age gap between us, and her assumed innocence didn't seem to align with my kinks. But in the end, none of that mattered. A connection stronger and more binding than my ropes brought us together, and I wasn't capable of resisting the pull. For all the reasons why we shouldn't be in a relationship, there are a dozen more that say we should.

She brings a sense of calm to my sometimes-war-torn troubled soul. She challenges me to be a better person in a way no one else dares, and everything feels lighter when her warm, brown eyes lock with my lighter blue ones. But most of all, she makes me feel loved for the first time in my life. Awakening emotions that I thought were dead long ago and opening my heart to a future that I never imagined could be possible.

On the mats, the girls pull apart, falling to lie on their backs. A thin sheen of sweat makes Charli's skin glow in the bright light and her chest heaves with exertion. She's so damn gorgeous; it takes my breath away, especially knowing that she's all mine.

I stroll over to stand beside her, offering my hand. She smiles that sweet smile she seems to save just for me as she places her slim fingers in my larger palm and I pull her up to standing, then into my arms.

"Oh, I'm all sweaty," she argues.

"That's how I like you," I whisper near her ear before burying my face into her neck and filling my lungs with the scent of her heated skin. She wraps her arms around my shoulders and her fingers dig into the hair on the back of the head.

"Shower?" she asks. As if she needs to.

"Hey, don't mind me. I'll just lie here a sweaty, exhausted wreck who just got her arse handed to her by her sister," Tori grumbles at our feet.

Laughing, I release an arm from Charli and offer Tori a hand to help her up.

She thanks me, then says to her sister, "You have gotten really good."

"I had a good teacher," Charli responds, tapping lightly on my chest.

"That's so not fair. I'll have to beg Tony to put some extra hours in training me." She strolls over to collect her bag, and with a goodbye casually tossed over her shoulder, she leaves.

"Let's shower upstairs in my apartment where we'll have some privacy," I suggest.

"Mmm ... Yes please," Charli agrees, seemingly just as eager for us to get naked.

I throw both of our bags over my shoulder, then taking her hand, lead her to the private elevator.

***

A little while later, I'm sitting on a stool at the main bar checking on a supplier delivery for Tony when Tori comes up behind me and places a hand on my shoulder.

A smile ticks up the corners of my mouth. "Where's your better half, Tori?" I ask, not even bothering to lift my head from my laptop.

"Damn you're good," she says with a smile in her voice.

This is the game she's been playing since Charli and I started dating, trying to trick me into mixing them up. She doesn't realize that what Charli and I have goes a lot deeper than how she looks. They may have been able to fool people in the past and me at least that first time, but not anymore.

My body recognizes Charli's in an elemental way that's pure chemistry. It's in the heat that emanates from a simple brushing of skin against each other or in the tight feeling I get in my chest just knowing she's nearby.

Every part of my being is finely tuned to her, in such a way that it's hard to explain to others. Charli gets it, but Tori still insists that I'll slip up one day. I know I won't, so I play along with her amusing attempts.

Charli's perfume reaches me, and I swivel on the stool. There she is.

She glides toward me like the beautiful angel she is, straight into my waiting arms.

Tori sighs loudly beside us. "I'm out of here. Not that you two would notice one way or the other." She goes to walk away, then turns back. "I nearly forgot. Ryan, can we chat later, when you haven't got your hands full with my sister?"

I look at Tori over Charli's shoulder. "Sure, anything wrong?"

A couple of months ago, Tori took over the role of gym manager. Her background in competitive sport combined with a business degree majoring in sports management made her a good fit. When Charli told me this soon after Tori arrived, a plan I'd had to expand the club's membership through the gym began to take shape. The three of us put together a business proposal and I presented it to my partners. Hunter agreed immediately, though Gio took a little longer to convince. I insisted that it had to be Tori running the gym as she had been part of the proposal and had the experience we needed. In the end, Gio's astute business mind overrode his personal reluctance to involve Tori in the business.

"No, it's all good. I've just had some ideas to increase usage of the gym, but it can wait. I'll see you guys later."

Dropping my head, I nuzzle into Charli's neck, filling my lungs with a breath of summer breeze, even though the city is well into fall outside, with the leaves on the trees displaying a mix of bright yellows, dark oranges, and muted golds.

"What are you doing down here?" she asks as her body melds closer with mine, her arms hooking loosely around my neck and my hands going to her hips where they belong.

"I'm waiting for you, so we can eat together."

"Don't you have manager-type things to do before we open?"

"Nothing as important as being with you."

She lightly slaps my chest. "You know you don't have to say things like that to get me into your bed."

"I know. But I like saying things like that to you." I stand but keep my hands firmly on her hips. "Come on, I've already had dinner delivered to my apartment."

We were only there an hour ago showering after the gym before she came downstairs to help Tony get ready for the club's opening. Since then, I've been working furiously to set up my surprise for her. I just hope she thinks it's a good surprise.

In the elevator, before we finish the short journey up to my apartment, I push the stop button and pull a blindfold from my back pocket.

Her eyebrow ticks up as she pops a hip and places her hand on it. "Is this going to be a kinky dinner?"

"No ... unless you want it to be," I suggest with a wink. "Really it's just I have a surprise for you."

"I love your surprises."

"And I love you. Now turn around so I can blindfold you."

"Yes, sir." Those two little words never fail to thicken my cock, and she knows it, based on the smirk painted across her lips. Her hands move to immediately clasp behind her back like she does when we play with ropes.

"No ropes tonight, angel."

"What a shame," she says, sounding disappointed. Charli seems to like playing with my ropes almost as much as I do. I've even been teaching her some of the simpler knots so she can try them out on me.

I tie the black silk scarf over her eyes, then swipe my keycard to take us up.

In my apartment, I lead her to the center of the living room. "Now wait here a minute while I do one more thing." I quickly run around lighting all the candles I laid out earlier.

"Okay I'm ready, you can take the blindfold off now."

She slides the blindfold up from her eyes, then blinks several times. "Oh my God, the room looks beautiful." She turns in a circle taking in all the string lights and candles illuminating the area. A small round table is set up to the side with a crisp, white linen cloth, plates, glasses, and flatware ready for dinner.

When she turns back to face me, her hand flies to her mouth. "Ryan, is this a proposal?" she gasps.

"What? No ... Well not yet."

"Oh." The smile slips from her mouth, and she pulls her bottom lip between her teeth, her cheeks flushing pink.

I rush to her side, wrapping my arms around her. "Sorry, I didn't think about how this would look. Fuck, I'm so shit at all this romantic stuff." I lean my forehead to hers. "I do want to marry you one day sweetheart but first I wanted to ask you to move in with me."

"You want me to move in with you?" she asks, her voice whisper soft, like she can hardly believe that's what I said.

"Absolutely. I wanted you to move in months ago, but I didn't want to rush you. I hate waking up without you beside me. I love you Charli and that means I want to share my life with you, fully and completely."

She flings her arms around my neck. "The answer is yes. One hundred percent, yes. I love you too."

Releasing one arm from her, I reach into my back pocket and pull out the keycard I had made for her, then hold it up. "Then this belongs to you."

Instead of taking the key, she places her hands on my cheeks and drags my lips to hers, sealing our agreement with a passionate kiss.

EPILOGUE

Charli

One Week Later

My clothes hang in Ryan's walk-in closet, taking up a pathetically small amount of real estate. But still, my heart feels full at the sight, one small symbol of Ryan and I merging our lives.

Sadie comes to stand beside me at the open double sliding doors. "Damn this is an amazing closet, I think my whole bedroom would fit into this vast space."

"Can't I just put my clothes right over there?" Tori asks from my other side. She points to the far end of the closet where Ryan cleared space for me, yet it still remains empty even after unpacking all of my clothes.

"I heard that, Tori." Ryan's deep voice comes from behind me, sending a familiar zap of pleasure up my spine even before he places his hands on my hips. "Besides, Charli will need that space to put the new dresses she'll be getting for the events we'll be attending over the holiday season."

"What events?" I spin in his arms.

"The ones I would like you to go to with me as my girlfriend." With a gentle finger under my chin, he closes my open jaw, then drops a featherlight kiss on my lips to seal them shut. "I'm sure Sadie and Tori will be happy to help you choose something and I'll give you my card to cover the cost. Don't worry, the invitations are not till December."

I open my mouth to protest, but again, he closes it with a kiss. "This is a work expense, so I'll cover the cost. Please, angel, I want you by my side." How does he even know what I'm thinking before I say it? And how can I refuse when he says please? Damn I love this man.

Bang! The sound of the elevator door opening echoes along the hallway.

"Who the fuck is that?" Ryan exclaims, already dropping his arms from around me and striding across the plush bedroom carpet before his heavy tread hits the wood flooring and pounds down the hallway. He looked ready to do battle with whoever has dared to enter his private domain.

But instead of the expected shouting, all we hear next is him saying, "What the fuck are you doing here?" in a tone that's measured and calm. A low, deep mumbled response doesn't help to confirm who the mysterious visitor is, other than it doesn't sound like a woman's voice. If it was, Ryan would have some explaining to do. It must be a friend, although he assured me earlier today that I'm the only person who he's given a keycard to.

If that's the case, who just let themselves into his apartment?

The three of us listen as a pair of slower, more measured footsteps tap toward the living room. We go to join them, but as I near the living room doorway, Ryan appears, blocking the entrance and reminding me of his man-wall impression from the first day we met. His gaze finds mine, then skips over my shoulder to Tori, who's standing behind me. Concern is etched into the crease between his brows and worry pulls the corners of his mouth down. His light-blue eyes have turned stormy.

What's wrong ... but I don't get to finish that thought before Gio appears behind him.

Tori's gasp is the only sound to break the chilly silence, but it's soon followed by an expletive slipping from Sadie's lips.

Ryan's gaze darts to mine, trying to send me a message that, for once, I don't understand because it's distorted by my concern for my sister. I step back in a futile attempt to block Gio from seeing my sister. It's too late and I turn in her direction, the ghostly gray of her skin tells me all I need to know. There is no way she wants to speak to him.

Gio sways toward her with a slurred word that I guess is meant to be *Bella*.

I cut him off before he can reach her. "Hey, buddy, how about you sit down before you fall." Hooking my arm into his, it doesn't take much to swing him in the opposite direction. Ryan is instantly on his other side. And I hear Sadie speaking quietly to Tori.

"Go to Tori," Ryan suggests, and I drop Gio's arm leaving Ryan to deal with him.

"I'm leaving," Tori says, some color returning to her cheeks and her voice firm.

"Tori?" Gio begs from where he's now slumped against the wall, one hand driving tracks through his thick, dark hair.

"Not now, Gio," Tori replies, cutting him off sharply. Her face now an expressionless mask. "If you want to speak to me, you need to sober up first." She then gives me a quick hug.

"I'll call you later," I tell her so only she can hear, then watch as she and Sadie leave.

I'm so proud of the way she stood up to Gio just now. The man has treated her badly. And while he appears to have suffered too, I'm glad she's not caving in to him.

Ryan coaxes Gio over to the sofa where he slumps back onto the cushions, then returns to my side. "I'm sorry, he's my friend and I can't turn him away."

"I know, I wouldn't ask you to," I say, resting a hand against his cheek.

"Charli, there's something else you need to know. Gio is also one of my silent partners. I'm sorry I should have told you sooner, but it just never came up." He drops his forehead to mine.

"It's okay." I lift his head up with both hands and place a kiss on his mouth. "Look, go help your friend and we can talk later in our bed."

"I love you," he tells me.

"And I love you too."

The End

Gio and Tori's story, Perfect Match is coming in August 2024.

CHARLI'S SIGNATURE COCKTAIL

Reposado tequila
Fresh pineapple juice, strained
Saffron Syrup
Lime juice

In a cocktail shaker with ice,
combine two ounces of reposado tequila,
and an ounce of saffron syrup.
Add 4 ounces of pineapple juice and a squeeze of lime.
Shake until very well-chilled,
Then strain into a chilled cocktail glass.

200   CATE LANE

ACKNOWLEDGEMENTS

This story hovered in the recesses of my imagination for a long while and would only pop into the forefront when the Carlson men visited The Vice Club for scenes in their books. Ryan and Charli's story was always meant to be told but it was a slow burn.

It started during the writing of Forbidden Lovers where Blake Carlson visits his friend Ryan at the club. That moment put my lead characters Ryan and Charli into my head, and they wouldn't leave before I'd written the scene where they meet on the steps. However, that's all it was one scene, until I was writing Satisfying the Billionaire with Hunter Carlson. He visited the club a couple of times and it had me wondering what bought Charli to the city and what-if she had a twin sister. Ryan and Charli's story evolved from those early scenes, and I honestly didn't know exactly where it would go until I was typing the words of their story. Looking back, I like where they ended up with their version of a perfect mix. I hope you do too.

There are so many people who help to bring my stories to life, and none more so than my family. Thank you to my husband and three adult children who keep me grounded when I'm stressing about deadlines. And to my niece, J.A. Low who is always there for a chat about covers, marketing or pretty much anything related to being an Indie author.

An equally important thank you goes out to the other members of my team. My new editor, Brooklyn, who is absolutely amazing at helping me to bring you the best story I can with all the emotion and steam, of course. And to Nicole, my proofreader, who reviews my final edits and bonus epilogues.

Thank you to my talented cover designer Kim Wilson, who has designed all the gorgeous covers for the series. And to Lou Stock for agreeing to do the formatting of this paperback to make it look pretty inside and out.

Finally thank you to my ARC team and my readers for choosing to read my story.

Cate xo

ABOUT CATE LANE

Cate Lane writes contemporary romance about swoony billionaire businessmen in custom-made suits, and hot military heroes, who find their HEA with strong independent women. All of her novels bring the heat and are standalone stories within an interconnected series.

She lives out her own happy ever after in Sydney, Australia with her husband and three children. When she's not writing, she likes to spend her time on beautiful beaches reading books or dreaming up new stories.

Sign up for Cate's newsletter to stay up to date on the latest news about new releases and bonus epilogues. Newsletter subscribers will be the first to receive the latest news, teasers and release information.
www.catelanebooks.com/newsletter

206   CATE LANE

ALSO BY CATE

The CARLSON DYNASTY series
Satisfying the Billionaire (Book One)
What happens when the satisfaction of a no-strings-attached lover ends up tying me in knots?
Maybe it's time for some rope play.

Eluding the Billionaire (Book Two)
Dealing with one arrogant author making demands on my time is all part of the job.
But when the author turns out to be my hot one-night stand, a publishing contract is the last thing I'm thinking.
And all I want to know is, *why did he leave that night*?

Seducing the Billionaire (Book Three)
What was I thinking?
Under duress, I agreed to let my sister's best friend stay in my spare room.
Only four weeks, she'd said. And that was twenty-eight days too long.

Gifting the Billionaire (A Christmas Novella)
Just friends ... Well, that's what I thought we were, until the night of the Carlson Christmas Charity Gala.

***

The LOVERS IN THE CITY series
Broken Lovers (Book One)
If heartache had a name, it would be Luke Steele ...

Forbidden Lovers (Book Two)
Some rules are meant to be broken.

Onetime Lovers (Book Three)
Maybe once will never be enough.
When One-time is so good they keep coming back for more.

Snowbound Lovers (A Christmas Novella)
Fireworks go off in the cold mountain air
of Aspen and it's not even New Year's Eve.

***

Made in the USA
Monee, IL
28 March 2025